Midnight Cartel

Chris Green

Lock Down Publications and Ca$h Presents

Midnight Cartel

A Novel by *Chris Green*

Chris Green

Lock Down Publications
P.O. Box 870494
Mesquite, Tx 75187

Visit our website @
www.lockdownpublications.com

Lock Down Publications
Like our page on Facebook: Lock Down Publications
@
www.facebook.com/lockdownpublications.ldp
Cover design and layout by: **Dynasty Cover Me**
Book interior design by: **Shawn Walker**
Edited by: **Jill Duska**

Stay Connected with Us!

Text **LOCKDOWN** to 22828 to stay up-to-date with new releases, sneak peaks, contests and more...

Thank you.

Submission Guideline.

Submit the first three chapters of your completed manuscript to ldpsubmissions@gmail.com, subject line: Your book's title. The manuscript must be in a .doc file and sent as an attachment. Document should be in Times New Roman, double spaced and in size 12 font. Also, provide your synopsis and full contact information. If sending multiple submissions, they must each be in a separate email.

Have a story but no way to send it electronically? You can still submit to LDP/Ca$h Presents. Send in the first three chapters, written or typed, of your completed manuscript to:

LDP: Submissions Dept
Po Box 870494
Mesquite, Tx 75187

DO NOT send original manuscript. Must be a duplicate.

Provide your synopsis and a cover letter containing your full contact information.

Thanks for considering LDP and Ca$h Presents.

Acknowledgments

This book means a lot to me, and I hope that everyone opens their mind to watch what's really going on. To understand this exciting and steamy story, you have to sink your time into this masterpiece. I'm getting better and better. Chris Green will be stamped in this world. Why? Because I was born to write. Who do I want to acknowledge in this book? Me. I'm thanking myself for waking up every morning, offering five prayers a day when no one else is praying for me at all, putting motivation and time into every book I make. I just want to be great, and I'm watching that dream happen while I'm going through one of the worst times of my life. I will stand by me and my craft, even if I don't have anyone else to do it. It's the reason I'm destined to win. No one can stop me because I'm the same person who has to fight for you all. My readers, family, friends, and Muslim brothers manda-tory. I love y'all and without me, I feel like there will be someone to let you all down. I won't let that happen on my watch. Peace, and Asalamu laikum.

Chris Green

Prologue

After making his way down the small staircase, Richard knocked sternly on the steel door. His black Armani dress shoes matched the all-black three-piece Tommy Hilfiger suit on his body. His smooth hair was greased to perfection and his jewelry gleamed with every slight movement.

He watched the eye latch slide back, and the door was quick-ly opened.

"Richard. Pleasure to see you, boss," the doorman greeted him with respect.

Replying with a nod, he continued into the room until he faced the ten board members. "I am so glad that you guys could make it tonight. We have exactly one minute before we get started." Richard stared at his timepiece.

As they sat in silence for the next sixty seconds, the timer on his watch beeped loudly. He walked over to the three men who were bound in separate chairs and removed the bag off the first man's head. His battered face was un-recognizable and he began to cough violently when the light pierced his eyes. Pulling his gun from his waist, Rich-ard placed a bullet in the chamber and blew his brains across the room.

Boom! The pistol roared inside of the small area.

"Next!" he mumbled, moving over to second man. "I under-stand that you're just a worker, so I'll give you a chance. Tell me what I need to hear." Richard waited with a smile like he was the Joker of Gotham.

"I swear it wasn't me. I-I would never even try it," he plead-ed.

His pleas were still unheard. Richard pressed the pistol against his right eye.

Boom!

Moving to the last man, he snatched the bag off more aggres-sively. "Cecil? I'm very disappointed in you. Out of everyone, I didn't expect you to let me down. How are we gonna handle this?"

"Fuck you, Richard. You gon' murder me anyway, mother-fucker. It doesn't matter what I tell you."

Boom! Boom! Boom! Boom!

"Don't tell me how the fuck I'm feeling right now, mother-fucker. Someone owes me answers, and I want them!" he shout-ed to Cecil's dead body.

After taking a deep breath, Richard glanced at his watch. Re-alizing that time was running behind, he took a seat at the table and wiped his hands with a napkin before handing the gun to one of his bodyguards.

"I'm glad that you were all able to make it. For starters, I have one question." He looked around at all the members of his table. "Where in the fuck is Raekwon?"

Chapter 1

It was a rainy Friday morning as Raekwon lay on his bottom bunk, awaiting his murder trial. He hadn't been able to sleep for the past four days because he knew that his life was coming to an end very soon. All he could do was ponder on Kimyetta and his child. Kim had been supporting him throughout his bid, but he knew that would come to an end once the judge slammed the gavel. He was so busy in the streets that he had nearly forgotten how to be a true family man, a man of honor who cherished his blood. Unfortunately, things were turning for a loop.

Within months, Raekwon became the reason Wilmington, Delaware had such a big rise in their murder rate, something that hadn't been seen since ten years prior. He bore a strict label of menace to society.

Rubbing his temple, he thought about his son Ryan. His foot-steps were treading in the same path since his conviction, and he was destined for a casket if his actions didn't turn to match the code of silence. But who could Raekwon blame? He was the one who taught his son the game, how to shoot a gun and sell dope. It was all in their genes, something that could never be passed if you wanted to lead their family throne. In the six years he was gone, he would hear the vicious rumors about his son creeping through the walls. On top of that, Kimyetta found cocaine in Ryan's closet, more than enough to get a grown man a life sentence.

Just as he finally dozed off to sleep, Raekwon was awakened by a guard yelling and popping cell doors.

"Fuck!" He slung his legs off the bed and slid on his two-piece jumpsuit.

Upon stepping out of the cell, Raekwon's eyes locked with a nigga named Solo. He was a huge black nigga that was slanging birds on the turf. His reputation in the free world was plotting on niggas in different states. His beady black eyes were a dead giveaway for that. He was a nigga that couldn't be trusted. He was also a Gangster Disciple from the motherland, the Dirty Chi town.

When it came to Raekwon, it was another story. He was nev-er the hunted. His pride wouldn't allow him to bite his tongue. Standing around silent was never an option. From the jail to the block, his pistol game was in the dirt league. Body bags were just a count after he reached murder number ten.

Looking into Solo's eyes, Raekwon nodded with a smile. "What's good, killa?" He folded his arms as if he was daring him for a challenge.

His size was intimidating. He stood 6'1" and weighed 265 pounds. Nothing but pure muscle. His dreads were thick and hung down to his shoulders. The aggressive look didn't match the humble person he pretended to be. He was mostly a hitta for the ones who played tough at the wrong times. The right fee would have you swimming through trash alley within a few hours.

"You the killer," Solo replied.

Raekwon was locked up for the murder of Solo's right hand man, Cecil. The word recently got back to the wrong mouth and after six years of laying low, they were finally face to face in the same prison.

"Make a move, homie. You gangsta, right?" Raekwon clutched his razor-sharp shank.

The dorm sensed the tension and began to step off of the big floor.

"I'ma see about you," Solo said, smiling. "We don't do police stunts. Everybody continue with y'all day. There's nothing to see," he spoke with authority.

"All right, ladies. Roll and fold. Make a line and let's move it," Officer Shields interrupted their dispute.

Solo and Raekwon quickly followed directions. They stepped into the line, and the entire dorm headed for the cafeteria. Their beef was far from over and the tension was about to spark faster than a match on gas. All he could do was wait.

* * *

614 W. 5th Street, Delaware

Groaning and flipping over from her loud alarm clock, Kimyetta turned to her nightstand and silenced her cell phone. The small framed picture of Raekwon and Ryan was facing directly towards her. After scrolling through the missed calls, she kissed the screensaver of her baby daddy. A million thoughts sped through her mind at once. She thought back to the summer of Raekwon taking them to the Bahamas for vacation. It was a blessing to feel those days, the times where the family was be-yond a limit. She reminisced on the good and bad moments, but it still equaled up to the same feeling.

After having the fancy clothes, diamonds, and foreign cars, her new destiny was to pull Raekwon out of that hell hole. They needed him back more than anything. A family was all she want-ed. Kimyetta never saw him as a notorious killer or drug dealer. He was only Raekwon Royal, a loving husband and a father that would kill before his family went without. In her eyes, he was still the honest, sincere, and loyal person she fell in love with, one that did his duties. Even though the love was strong, the prison time was severing a bond that was barely hanging.

Kimyetta had grown up in the projects of Riverside. It was down in the back on Bower Street. Her mother, Elma, was a strong individual who raised her to be strong, determined, and sophisticated. She believed in men working to feed the house. Her structure and mind frame was solid, but sometimes a bit harsh.

Growing up, she never knew her father. After she met Raekwon at the age of sixteen, he showed Kimyetta a life that she never knew existed. It was usual for him to flex his large dope boy paper. He would pull up in a Benz on Tuesday. Wednesday it would switch to a Range. He was unpredictable to be so young, but his hustle was like no other. Raekwon wasn't the average eighteen-year-old teen. He was highly dangerous, and that was proved early in his time of destruction.

If a man even looked at Kimyetta once, he was applying pres-sure. It was his way of keeping her protected and secured. Kimyetta had witnessed him kill for the pettiest things. He would only tell her that it was about the respect. It was a blessing to be feared, but more of a gift to be respected. It was all chess to him. It was hard to communicate in the streets when everybody feared that her man would come to execute the whole block. Every hood had its own don. Riverside birthed the killa named Beast. The west side raised Maurice, better known as Moe. The north side was held down by Raekwon Royal, the Grim Reaper of the entire city. Beast and Moe were dead and gone. That left him terroriz-ing alone through the late night streets of Delaware.

Everything that Kimyetta was going through at the time was an adjustment. Raekwon taught her the techniques of the streets before he left. That was all she held on to. The recipe for success. After giving birth to her son, Ryan Royal, she put the streets behind her and turned into a pampered housewife. Having a son only made Raekwon grind harder, even if that meant picking up the burner to make it happen. He was there for Kim. Day in and day out. Of course, after she gave birth, he started to lose interest in her and began to slide around with the baddest of the city. Raekwon began to act strange and it was a clear sign that she was no longer worthy as a wife. Raekwon was caught cheating nu-merous times and created heated fights, disputes which left her with no choice but to leave him. Calling quits on their marriage, she gave him back his ring and stepped away.

A few of Raekwon's associates were constant problems with-in their relationship also. Instead of doing the original plan of family time, he crossed her and Ryan out for his right hand man Tommie, the one who constantly landed him in a cell time after time. He had more influence than the most. His grimy ways were natural habits and there was never a great day when he was around. It was the same with his friend, Rasheed. They all formed together some weak-ass alliance of getting money. It tore down the dream of Kimyetta having her moment, and that caused her to be furious. His absence with smashing bitches was on the regular. Eventually, Kimyetta grew tired and flipped the cards. Sex wasn't enough when she crept out with Tommie. It grew bigger when Rasheed wanted in on the action. Instead of being loyal friends, they decided to have their way with Raekwon's woman, a dark secret that was never supposed to surface.

The deceit towards Raekwon was eating at Kimyetta's mind. After telling him that she slept with his two partners in crime, he snapped into a rage. He never hit her for any reason, but that day caused him to go a bit overboard. Instead of harming her, he set out to have an emergency meeting with his two slime brothers.

Checking into a hotel, Raekwon murdered them both with three shots to the face each. They were found days after his rampage. That was a day she would never forget. That night, she received the beating of her life. She was nearly killed, which placed Raekwon behind Hayes state prison for three long years. After coming home, Kwon had a different look at life. He even converted to Islam to find more patience and guidance.

Raekwon's relationship with Kimyetta had faded. The only thing that shared their time was Ryan. She had already found a man by the time he was free, Deandre, the cool man everybody knew as Dre. He was a hardworking man that owned an electri-cian business. He loved Kimyetta and definitely paid homage to the family with his earnings. Kimyetta was never in it for the money because she truly felt that she shared a bond with her new companion, but after his habit flipped for cocaine, things started to change.

After experiencing a change with Dre, Kimyetta began to call Raekwon to reason out their disputes. Happiness wasn't flowing with her and shit was crashing to the ground. She needed help. The statement of him being there forever rested in her mind. That's what she always held on to.

Coming inside the house one night, Dre reeked of alcohol and cigarettes. His work bag rested on his shoulder and a bottle of Jack Daniels was hanging from his hand.

"Dre. Are you okay?" She walked over to him with worry.

In the snap of an eye, he was whaling blows down on her head. Ryan watched on in horror because he was too little to pick a fight with a full-blown junkie. Running to his bedroom, he dialed his father's number on the house phone.

"Hello?" Raekwon answered.

"Dad. This man hitting my mom. You need to come do some-thing about this. I'm tired of it."

"What you talking about, Dre and yo' mama?"

"Yeah."

"I'm on the way right fucking now. Stay there."

Driving down Vincent Circle, Raekwon reached Kimyetta's house in a matter of minutes. Without a word, he walked into the house and let his Desert Eagle speak for him.

Boom!

The first slug ripped through Dre's head, causing Kimyetta to jump with a light scream. The second bullet blew through his back. Running down the steps, Ryan watched as his daddy placed one last slug through Dre's brain.

Raising his head to face Kimyetta, Raekwon smirked. "Since you can't handle being with a nigga, you should be just fine alone. Ryan, pack you and your mother's shit. Y'all moving tonight."

Snapping out of her trance, Kimyetta stood up from the bed. After straightening the picture frame on the night stand, she released her brown hair and placed her silk robe on. Heading for the bathroom, she took care of her personal hygiene and quickly showered.

Within thirty minutes, she was dressed and ready to start her day. Pushing into the kitchen, she prepared a hefty breakfast like every morning: hash browns, biscuits, sausage, and waffles. Her stove was never full enough for Ryan's large appetite .He was just like his father. Still, it was her duty to serve for the men of her household.

Retiring back for the couch until she had to leave, Kimyetta ate her breakfast while watching reruns of the TV series The Game.

* * *

12 p.m. Eastside 9th Pine, Delaware

As he walked down Ninth and Pine, Ryan's hoodie was tied tightly around his face. He clutched on the .38 special that aligned the rim of his jeans. Moving at a fast pace, he stared at all the familiar faces from either school or the hood. Getting to Kirkwood Street, Ryan spotted his target, the cap a dollar from everyone on the block dopeboy Keem. He was booming weight on 10th and Bennitt. It had been a few weeks and his homework was about to come in handy. The payday was well-needed.

Walking into the corner store on Ninth, Ryan made his way into the alley beside the building. Traffic was known to pump heavily after the evening rush hour. It would be just enough movement for him to pull his caper without being noticed. Wait-ing patiently for his lick to walk out, Keem exited the store and headed straight for the alley. Just as he turned the corner, Ryan shoved the barrel of his revolver into Keem's mouth.

"Waitttt!" he screamed with his hands in the air. Keem's eyes were widened in fear and it wasn't long before he received his complimentary slap from Ryan's gun.

"Shut the fuck up, nigga! Hand that shit over, bitch." He quickly ran Keem's pockets. Taking the small bankroll, he confis-cated the dub bags of crack. "Where the rest of it?"

"Bro, that's it. I'm doing bad out here. Don't kill me 'bout the li'l drugs, young bull."

"You lying. I seen you come in the alley four times today. Give it to me or I'ma kill your stupid ass!" He clicked the ham-mer of his strap back.

Taking a moment to see if he wanted to buck the bullet, he gave in. "It's under the rock. The one next to the garbage can."

Sliding over to the spot, he pushed the medium boulder over. A nice roll of money sat perfectly on a big bag of heroin packs and at least ten thousand in drugs. He snatched it up, shoved it into his pocket, and aimed his gun over to Keem.

"Get the fuck up and run, pussy. If you come back on Ninth, I'm killing yo' dumb ass." Ryan let off three warning shots.

Boc! Boc! Boc!

Keem wasted no time scrambling to his feet. Breaking down the alley, he lowered his head, moving faster than a cheetah. Moving the opposite way, Ryan headed straight for Chestnut Street. Ryan was laughing and trying to catch his breath at the same time. By the time he stopped running, he knew that the coast was clear.

Walking down to Rodney Square, he pulled out the bag he tucked into his Nike pullover pocket. Glancing inside at the knots of dope, Ryan counted and estimated a total of

$9500 in product. The bills were easy to count. In five minutes, Ryan thumbed through his new bankroll. Adding up twelve thousand in hun-dreds, he smiled.

After tucking the money back in his pocket, Ryan threw the drugs in his bag. He slid over to Market Street, checked his G-shock, and dropped a few bands in Sneakervilla. Snatching up a few pants and T-shirts to stall some time, he decided to head back for the hood. Ryan knew that his mother was probably gonna call the school, but teachers couldn't show you how to cop that bag like Ryan did. School just wasn't his thing. The only purpose of going was the freaky girls and lunch. Teaching him anything was gonna bounce off the wall because he surely wouldn't be around by second period.

Ryan stood 5'8" with red skin, and his hair was curly and low. His face structure made him and Raekwon look more like twins than father and son. He was cut with mus-cle from the daily workout he enforced on himself. Ryan was another innocent face that would easily trick you into the devil's pen, a young pretty boy who received panties by the dozen, teens to grown women.

After Ryan got to sixth grade, he began to slack in school. His habit of smoking and skipping class was in full effect. All he wanted to do was live up to the life of his dad and hang with his crew, D.J, Wicked, and Reckless.

Rocking with the hard hittas of the entire school, they became top priority in no time. The crew dressed to impress daily. This lasted the entire way until the boys touched high school. By this time, their young crew was feared through-out the north and south of Delaware. After the boys' fresh-man year, they were all push-ing the movement of robbing for the dough. Ryan was the head of laying the pistol down. It became his daily job to make sure the plot went as smoothly as possible. It was the only way to become the head of Delaware.

Reckless and Wicked were cousins from the city of Phoenix, Arizona. Down in their area, murder was an understatement. The two of them alone caused havoc in the small city. It was all gravy to make money, but not good to trust a motherfucker. Their dark complexions were even and they both shared the same Mad Max hairstyle: dreaded at the top, bald on the sides. Their weight ranged around 140 pounds, but both of their trigger fingers added up for the rest. Wicked was smoother and the oldest. He was wiser than everyone expected, more than his cousin, who lived up to his name.

DJ, on the other hand, was the opposite. He could rage out and snap like the rest, but he was more collected and brilliant. He was always calm and played shit smart. Instead of dropping out like the rest of them when they started to get money, DJ still stayed in school. He only spoke when necessary and was mature, and all of his movements played a part in the team winning. In all, Ryan searched for the best group of niggas to get money with. There was no better feeling. After his dad fell to the prison system, he grew as a man. He knew for sure that if he continued to keep his game tight, the throne would be his very soon.

Chris Green

Chapter 2

It was later that night when Ryan decided to treat the boys with the free paper he earned earlier. After all, if he had it, they had it. There was never such a thing as them going without. Sliding through the shopping stores, he skinned down for shoes and other items until he was loaded with bags. Making his way inside the clothing store with DJ by his side, Ryan purchased different brands of clothing. A peanut butter-complexioned woman with almond-shaped eyes walked over to him. Her body was nice and tight. The clothing she wore showed her sexy figure to the T. A white Gap T-shirt hugged her juicy breasts and the khaki shorts on her butt exposed her smooth legs. Dimples had a home inside of her chunky cheeks and her smile was impeccable. She had Ryan starstruck for a slight second.

"Hey. Do you need any help?" Her tone was so sweet.

"Yeah. We can head to the counter."

Reaching the register, the associate stared at all the merchan-dise. "You gotta be a baller coming in here shop-ping like this."

"I'm not a baller. I'm on a budget, ma." He smiled. "Where are you from?"

"North Philly."

"Word? Where at in Philly?" Ryan asked curiously.

"Germantown Ave. Born and raised. I'm just going to college right now and I didn't want to be in my city for school. This is my side job."

"What's your name?" he responded after she finished bagging his things.

"What, you can't see?" She pointed at her nametag, which read Precious.

"Precious, huh? My name is Ryan. You ain't never heard of me? Rich and Royal committee, baby."

Laughing, she looked at him with a raised brow. "No, but I see that you surely gonna let me know. How old are you, Ryan?"

"Seventeen."

"Wow! You don't look young. You could've went for twen-ty-three. All this money at seventeen. Where do you work, so I can come apply?"

"I don't think you wanna work with me." He smirked, hand-ing her the money for his merchandise.

"Yo, Ryan. Wicked and Reckless waiting on us. They out-side," DJ said before moving toward the exit.

"Cool."

Turning his face back to Precious, he grinned. "I'm saying. It gotta be a way I can get your number to see what type of busi-ness you can help me with, since you worried about my money?" Ryan asked.

"Mm-hmm. I can help you in a few places. That's if you're willing to listen. You look like you're smart. Maybe I can give you a few lessons of management and invest-ment when you have the chance." She wrote her number on the back of his receipt. Sliding it to him, she waved her fingers.

"I'ma make sure I use this."

"Please do," Precious responded before he could walk off.

Glancing at his watch, he saw that it read 2:01, which meant he had thirty minutes before school let out. He walked over to 5th Washington and sat on the church steps with his crew. Wait-ing for the small time to pass by, he thought about his dad. Raekwon was hardly ever able to get visitation because he was always in the hole. Soaking up all the game from his pops, he learned quickly to save shit for a rainy day. There was no telling when shit was gonna go sour. It was all a part of his ambitions as a hustla. Ryan didn't know why, but the love for money was all that mattered when it came to surviving. Bustas couldn't fuck with the team, so the rest was too worthless to think about.

Checking the time, Ryan saw it was time to head back for the school. "Y'all niggas come on. We can slide back. They should be letting out in a minute." Ryan grabbed all of his bags.

"I'm saying. Are we still kicking shit tonight or what?" DJ asked.

"Of course."

"Y'all know we ain't winning with this walking shit," Wicked said with all his shit. "We look like some bums, man."

"That shit won't be for long. I'm just done with riding in hot-ass cars. We need to be legit. Everything should be good by the weekend."

Making it back to Newark High School, Ryan approached his girlfriend, Faith. Grabbing her slim waist, he placed a kiss on her lips.

Setting the bags on the ground, DJ wiped his forehead. "Damn! It's hot as fuck."

"Where have you been? I was going crazy, boy." Faith play-fully hit him on the chest.

"Out and about." He looked into her sparkly brown eyes.

Standing 5'4", Faith was high yellow with a petite body. Her hair hung down to the middle section of her back. It was all natural and dark brown. Faith would put you in the mind of Ariana Grande. She was adventurous and fun, and also educated and loyal. She was Ryan's keeper. Her hot pink lips were another attraction for her swimsuit model face. The fact they were having sex started to curve her figure just right. It started slowly and began to escalate to a mandatory session by the night. She was a full professional and he was her first.

"Look, I need you to take this to your house for me. Give me a minute to go home and I'ma slide through." Ryan handed her all his bags.

"What? You're not coming now?" Her entire facial expression changed.

"I can't. You know I gotta get this lady off my back. Just be easy and I'll pull through." He kissed her lips.

Rolling her eyes, Faith grabbed the bags and headed for the school bus. Turning around to greet the fellas, Ryan showed them all some love before peeling off to hear Kimyetta's mouth.

As he walked towards his apartments, Wicked and Reckless moved the opposite way with DJ. It didn't take long for him to hit the back street to reach his block. Moving through his apart-ment complex, he entered the crib and headed straight for his room. Just as he closed his bedroom door, he could hear Kimyetta stepping down the hallway. The loud banging on his room door forced him to take a deep breath. As she busted through his door, Ryan went through her usual scare tactic. He looked his mother in the eyes.

"Where the fuck you been, motherfucker?" Her pupils were red with a blaze of anger.

"I was at school."

"Think twice. Speak once. Don't fucking lie to me, Ryan. Where have you been? You know I was gonna call and check behind you, boy. I wasn't playing when I said that I would kick your ass out. Do you think I was play-ing?" she yelled aggressive-ly.

"Nah. I heard you, Mama," he said calmly before lying down on the bed.

"Get the fuck up when I'm talking, bitch! Show some fucking respect!"

Ryan looked at her and did what was asked of him.

"Boy, don't disrespect me in my own house. You don't pay no bills around this bitch. I pay the cost to be the boss. You think you doing something because yo' punk-ass girl-friend giving you the allowance she worked her ass off for? How about worrying with school and getting your attend-ance up before your ass be in the pen like your daddy? Y'all motherfuckers gonna be directly in a cell next to each other. Keep it up." She pointed her finger angrily.

Drifting off to the night before last on how he and Faith made love in Kimyetta's bed, he burst into a fit of laughter.

"You see something funny, Ryan?"

"Nah, Mama. I'm just tired. You always do this to me."

"I should backhand yo' stupid ass." She held her hand in the air. "Yo' ass cooking my dinner tonight and I want the kitchen cleaned." Kimyetta stormed out of his room.

The love that Faith and Ryan shared was something Kimyetta didn't believe in. Her past left her stuck on a mis-ery train that she was never able to recuperate from. She always warned him that love was fake and it only lasted for a moment. Just enough to share a memory of something that would never last. She didn't feel a relationship was good for her baby boy, especially when he needed to focus on taking care of his Queen. After all, she was the one who would forever hold the throne.

* * *

Reidsville State Prison

"Pick that fuck nigga up!" Raekwon said as he clutched onto his knife. He stared down at Solo's bloody face. After gym call, he slipped and came back to the dorm too quick. Little did he know that four of Raekwon's Muslim brothers were paid to handle that business for his slick tongue.

"I never had intentions on getting at you, dawg. That's real street talk." He panted with a lack of oxygen. "I only got twenty months left. I don't wanna die before I got the chance to make it home to my family," Solo pleaded.

"You got twenty months, huh?" Raekwon folded his arms as his brothers held Solo up by his throat and arms.

"Yeah, bruh. I didn't want no drama. That's what I'm telling you."

"Mmm. Nigga, I got life. I'm looking at the death penalty. You think I give a fuck about your twenty months or yo' fuck-ass kids, nigga? I'ma die in this bitch. I got one son, nigga, and you about to feel all his pain," Raekwon said, with spit flying every time he spoke.

Feeling the rage build, he slammed a six inch knife through Solo's eye. "Pussy motherfucker! Who you gon' see about, nigga?"

Solo cried in agony as one of the brothers covered his mouth.

"I warned you once," Raekwon whispered into his ear before pulling the screwdriver from his face.

"Ahhhh!" His scream was surely being heard by the guards who sat inside the control panel.

As Raekwon forced the screwdriver into Solo's other eye, he could feel the back of his head press against his weapon. Solo fought against the pain, but was not able to beat the strength of the strong men. He released a turd directly in his state pants.

"Stay still, bitch!" Raekwon shouted.

As the smell of his bowels released in the air, he stepped to the side and watched as his brothers plowed their shanks into Solo's abdomen, face, and throat. His brother Hakim from south D.C. finished off the job and placed an ice cold razor across his throat. Within two seconds, blood was covering the cell and Solo's last breath was being taken.

"Now you can be with ya boy Cecil in the afterlife," he spat before the men exited the room. Shutting the door behind them, they all headed back out for the rec yard.

* * *

After the lockdown process occurred, Raekwon sat in his cell, hoping that the snitches didn't rat out his recent altercation with Solo. There were no cameras at the prison camp, so everything that came out came from the police-ass inmates across the com-pound. After seeing the GBI leave out of the building, he took a deep breath.

Thinking about his son Ryan, he knew that his legacy would live on. It was the only thing that gave him an ounce of hope despite the thought of the white man executing him. When he came to think about it, Raekwon taught his son nothing that would help benefit him in life besides busting a gun for protec-tion. He was only doing what his father and deceased older brother did to him.

Raekwon never chose this life; he was forced into it. His fa-ther, Jamal Red Johnson, the notorious kingpin in Camden, New Jersey, introduced Kwon and his brother

Ryan to a life of crime which eventually became his career. His older brother was gunned down the same day of little Ryan's birthday. It was the reason he shared a close bond with his son through all the years in chain gang.

Raekwon's dad didn't last very long in the game. It was natu-ral for a man to reach his demise after starving the entire hood. He was gunned down and robbed for everything by his own associates. Raekwon and Ryan sought revenge over their father's death, but still came up short. The murder game was being laid down and they were stacking the money while doing it. There wasn't enough brains and too much muscle. While Ryan was the obnoxious and loud type, Raekwon earned the respect from his name. His quietness is what the people feared more than any-thing. After all the loud talk, Ryan was found dead after a drug deal gone wrong. He was stripped and beaten to death before catching a slug through the head. It was the day Raekwon's heart turned cold.

Barely five years apart, he'd found himself burying his father and brother. He began to torture niggas to mark the line on his territory. Then one day he met someone that calmed his spirit, Kimyetta. She was the one he showed a different life. She de-served to be treated well because her love stretched a million miles. That was the only thing pushing him to get home. It was hard to stamp your name in the hood, only to see it be taken away with ease.

Grabbing his headphones, he placed them over his ears and eased back. Tupac's song, "Keep Ya Head Up," crooned smooth-ly through the speakers. All Raekwon wanted at that time was to sit with his young son before it was too late.

* * *

Westside 5th and Monroe

As Ryan sat on the steps of the vacant house, he laughed with DJ and this old head, Cheek Raw. They passed the Kush back and forth while talking shit about the hood. West Fifth Street was the spot where they grew up and built a name for themselves. Ryan and DJ learned most of their trickery and gunplay mentality from Cheek Raw. Dude was more of a mentor, a professor with being a goon. It was his hustle. He showed them what it took to get money and earn respect. He was a twenty-three-year-old hustla who was known around the city, but hated by many. His murder game was placed down at the age of sixteen and it'd been established not to test his gangsta. Due to his size, he was often not taken seriously. Learning over time that he was beyond crazy, his status rose through the neighborhood. Cheek Raw always made sure that Ryan and DJ were straight, from the money in their pockets to the guns on their hips. He was a loud and flashy cat, but his money matched his loud taste. His jewels were top notch and the women threw themselves at him on a daily basis. Even after all of that, he was smart. No one knew where he was resting his head.

"Hey, Cheek. You holding?" A woman moved over to them. She was white with blonde hair and her head was wrapped in a stitched Philly skullcap.

"What you need, Sindy? I'm not doing no credit."

"But who else am I gonna go to, Cheek? My check don't hit 'til Wednesday. I been straight all day," she whined with a sick look.

Digging in his pocket, he handed her a fifty sack of dope. "I want a hundred on Wednesday. Don't make me look for yo' ass either."

"Never. I'm always on time. See y'all later." She rubbed a hand through his curly hair. "Bye, Ryan."

"Bye, Sindy." Ryan passed the blunt over to DJ.

"But anyway, y'all, listen to this. I got a little lick for y'all." Cheek caught both of their attention.

"Oh, word? What you talking?" Ryan asked with itchy hands.

"A couple grand. Some y'all could use and make good on."

"Shit. How good?" DJ rose to his feet.

"A nigga out in brown town got a mean li'l trap spot. I shopped with him a few times. Young bull bitch made. I'm talking cold-blooded pussy. It be like three niggas in there every time I swing through. He on some dumb shit though. I came in the spot and scoped all these fools' business. After I showed 'em a few dollars, he got too comfortable with me. I know what all they got in there, from top to bottom."

"Just give me and DJ the address. We will handle the rest. But are you sure this nigga cool? Because I won't hesitate to slump that kid. It's zero tolerance for me, Cheek. You know how I move," Ryan stated with his hands inside the thick nice sweats.

"You know I'll never lie to you, young bull. I'll swerve y'all around there tonight to scope shit out for yourself," he replied as they both stood up to give him some dap. Ryan and DJ threw their hoods on before departing.

"11:00 on the dot. Hit my phone, and bring y'all hammers with y'all." Cheek walked away.

Chapter 3

Heading over to nearest pizza joint, the boys stepped inside to soak up a small amount of heat before making the walk back to the block. Ryan turned his phone on just as they touched a seat-ing booth.

"Yo. I'm 'bout to order this shit to go. By that time, you should be all warmed up and shit, nigga." DJ headed for the counter.

Before Ryan could make a call on his phone, Faith's number popped up on his front screen. Without hesitation, he answered.

"Yo! What's good, baby?" He leaned back in his chair, smil-ing.

"Where you at? And whose number you got on this re-ceipt?" She questioned.

"I'm in Adams pizza place, and that's my cousin num-ber. Chill out, ma."

"A'ight, I hear you, boy. What you doing at Adams any-way?"

"I'm eating, Faith, damn. Wassup with all the ques-tions? You interrogating me now?" His voice showed the annoyance he was feeling. "I'm just with DJ. We just laid back." He sipped on the grape Fanta DJ placed on the table.

"I hear you. I thought you was coming over?"

"I am. I just had to chop it up with Cheeks before I made my way over. Get ready for me."

"Boy, stop. We ain't doing nothing tonight. Besides, my mom and dad are here. I'm not even done with my re-port for school. You gotta start and finish without me, buddy." Faith laughed.

"Yeah, whateva." Ryan licked his bottom lip.

"Aww…what's the matter? That didn't hurt your feelings, did it?"

"I'm straight. You can't hurt me with no booty. It's already mine, Faith," he stated with confidence.

"No, seriously though, baby. I've been having cramps lately. Plus, I've been sleeping a lot. Too much studying has me over-loaded and I don't know if that's where this pain is coming from."

"That's your problem, Faith. You try and think too much, bae. You gotta relax your mind."

"You right. Call my phone when you get over this way so I can open the door for you."

"Cool."

After hanging up, Ryan looked at DJ heading for him with their food in hand. "You ready to roll out? We got a long day tomorrow."

"Word. Let's do it."

* * *

As Faith lay on her bed, she tried to think about how she would break the news to her mom and dad about the pregnancy. Her school résumé was untouchable. It was their last year of high school and college was knocking on the door. She knew that it would probably be a shocker for them both, but it wasn't inten-tional. Perhaps the child would keep Ryan out of the streets. It was the same reason she still hadn't told him anything.

Walking into her bedroom, Faith's mother reached for the light. "Girl, you alright in here? It's all dark and stuff. What's wrong, baby?" She could see the worry written on her daughter's face.

Wiping a tear from her cheek, she nodded. "I'm okay. It's just that I think…I don't know. Ryan just been acting fishy lately."

"What? You're sitting in here crying about Ryan? Baby girl, he's a good kid and all. I mean, I love him like one of my own, but you're going to meet a million other Ryans. Don't stress yourself out. Especially over teenage love. You're too young for that," Ms. Anderson explained.

Consumed in her own thoughts, Faith remained silent. Her mom just didn't understand. Ryan was her everything. Her first love, best friend, and also the only person that truly listened to her. Ryan played a major role in her life that couldn't fade off for nothing.

Of course, Ryan was known to be with some groupies on the side, but everyone damn sho' knew where she stood with him. Ryan was the first person to ever touch her. That alone meant a lot.

"Yeah. You're right, Mama," Faith replied with a fake smile.

So much for telling her about the pregnancy. Faith was bound to go off the hinges just from that small conversation right there. As she continued to nap her life away, Faith began to think about how Ryan would take the news of his growing seed. Even the thought of how they had to take care of a newborn child had her mind thinking of all the possible negativity that was bound to come

"You hear me, girl?" her momma asked, breaking the deep trance.

She was so engaged with her own thoughts that she never paid attention to the conversation her mom was actually speaking on.

"Alright, Ma." She rolled over on her stomach.

Listening to the bedroom door open and close, Faith reached over for her phone to check the Facebook app. Before she could media surf, she received a phone call from Ryan.

"Hello," she answered.

"Aye yo. I'm on my way over there. You need to come out-side."

"Okay. Here I come."

"A'ight."

"No. Don't hang up. I wanna hear yo' voice." Faith smiled.

"I'm on 4th, girl. I'm about to be around there. Chill out." He ended the call.

"Rude bastard."

Walking to her closet, she put on her Northface jacket and a pair of white Air Max's. Moving downstairs, she opened the front door. The cold, blistering wind took her by surprise.

"Shit!" Faith shivered before crossing her arms. Scanning the block for Ryan, she squinted her eyes, but couldn't see any movement. Just as she was about to turn inside, he turned onto Madison. The black Nike track suit he wore hid his identity, but Faith could notice her love from anywhere.

Blowing her breath into her palms, Faith tried to disguise her bright smile. The thought of her child came to mind as he got closer. She didn't want to hide the situation from him, especially when the trust level was past one hundred.

As he approached her steps, they embraced, and Ryan's touch immediately warmed Faith. "Wassup, love." His lips connected with hers for a short kiss.

"We got a lot to talk about, Ryan." She looked into his eyes.

"Aw shit. What happened? You only say my name like that when you're upset."

Following her into the house, she led him to the couch. "Sit down. I'm about to adjust the heat."

Stepping over to the thermostat, Faith turned the knob and headed back over to him. Sliding down next to him, Ryan gazed at her curiously. "You a'ight? What's going on? You know I don't like when you do that shit."

"I'm good. Don't you think that it's about time for you to leave the streets alone? Ain't shit out there for you, Ryan."

Faith's heart was beating quickly and she didn't want to just jump in with the talk about their baby. From the look on his face, he was expecting her to argue about another freak or being around the sluts of Delaware.

"Baby, what are you talking 'bout? You know this how I eat. Where you going with this? Because we don't normally speak about stuff like this."

"Ryan, I love you. I don't want shit to happen to you out there in them grimy streets. Your mother loves you. But my heart still has to wonder if I will ever get a call about you being taken away."

Ryan sat up and listened to his girl closely. He knew that she was very passionate about family, so it was always a serious matter.

"It's a bloodbath in them neighborhoods, and I just don't want you to fall victim. You hardly ever answer the phone, so you leave me no choice but to be worried. You're not even going to school anymore. Ever since you've been with DJ, Reckless, and Wicked, you've changed." She rolled her eyes.

"Real talk, Faith, I'm out here grinding, trying to make this dough for us."

"Us? Nigga, you doing that shit for you because I have never asked you for anything but your sweet love. Boy, bye." She waved him off with an attitude.

"Chill, man."

"No. Because you're never serious about shit that I say. I hope you're around to see me give birth to our child. That's what's real."

Her voice was so loud that she nearly forgot her parents were upstairs.

"Baby? Is that what this is about? You pregnant?" Ryan raised off the couch to look at her.

"That's what I said." Tears were welling in her eyes. "What you gon' do now, Ryan? We got a child. I'm not killing it. Abor-tion is nowhere in the picture."

"I'm not asking you to. That's some coward shit. I'ma take care of mine. Real talk," he stated with assurance. Grabbing her into a hug, he stroked her face gently.

Faith's mind was spinning on how Ryan took the news so well. "Are you serious, Ryan? You're not mad?"

"Mad for what? We finna be grown about this. I knew what I was doing when we had sex. It's a part of it. Don't feel like you trapped me or I trapped you. It takes two to make a baby," he spoke softly.

Faith nodded to his pleasing words.

Ryan placed a finger under her chin. "I love you. I don't care about the rest of them girls. They all came and went like the money I've spent. We've been through it all, but I'm gonna stand regardless. We good on everything be-cause that's my job. I want to be with you for the rest of my life. I mean what I say and I say what I mean. It's no way around me. Never hold shit back from me. Stay true and don't keep secrets. I love you regardless. The same way I'm gonna cherish my kid." Ryan kissed her again.

Faith couldn't help but admire the handsome young man she grew to love. He was the absolute best. Even though his mouth and mind would outweigh his heart sometimes, he was still special with flaws attached.

The thoughts of his father crossed her mind and she knew that he was a splitting image of the man her dad once ran the streets with. It was said that Raekwon would throw barbeques for the entire neighborhood. He was good on taking care of the elderly. All the original made men in the hood would speak highly of Raekwon, so it was a must for his son to live up to the same actions.

Hours eventually passed and the sun faded along with the horizon. Their laughs and debates on the child came to a halt when the sound of Faith's mother's bedroom door opened. Hearing the footsteps head for the stairs, they sat up correctly.

Markie D reached the living room floor and glared at them both. Faith's dad was a true hood star himself. Before he could drown in the pits of Delaware, he signed away for the U.S. Marines after having a death spree with Ryan's father. He retired and placed his time into taking care of Faith. He was definitely overprotective because she was his only child. It was the nature of a father.

However, the respect for Raekwon is what allowed Ryan to even step an inch close to his daughter. His only rules were to never mislead her or mistreat his child as if she was a gutter girl and of course show respect with his hands. Besides that, he wasn't on the strict dickhead shit. He was more laid back.

"Ryan. Wassup, kid, what you been up to?"

Smiling, he leaned up. "Nothing much, Markie. Just taking it easy, man."

"How's school going, man? I heard this is y'all last year?" He tossed on his thin fleece jacket.

"You know I'ma keep it real. I'm lacking, but I'm striving," Ryan admitted. Faith giggled silently.

"Man, get ya head right. Put the full course effort into them books. If yo' dad had a chance, I bet he would love to see that again. It would make him happy."

The statement was surely accurate, and he couldn't lie. The dreams of finishing school would be great. It just wasn't meant at that time. Hearing the old head speak about what they could have done back in the day was just another sad-ass story that he wasn't up to hear. Who the hell was willing to work a nine to five when the streets pumped that yearly salary in a month? Mickey D's wasn't a fucking option. Before he slaved for minimum wage of $8.50, he would slang crack until the age of eighty-three in order to take care of Faith and his little one.

"See, the youth just don't understand. Y'all are the future. We supposed to be taken care of by y'all. The military taught me that," he said with a stupid expression.

"Daddy. The military has nothing to do with the kids. They don't care about that. The army wants you to take care of your country. Nothing else for the land of the free," Faith joked with a small salute.

"See. That's the why y'all will never get to my age. You too stubborn." Markie D shook his head and gave Ryan a handshake before leaving out of the front door.

After kicking shit with Faith for another thirty minutes, Ryan checked the time. Standing to his feet, he grabbed his jacket. "Aye yo, baby. I'm about to go handle something. I'll be calling your phone." He placed a kiss on her cheek.

"Be safe." She smirked, catching a quick attitude.

Ignoring that, Ryan made his way out into the thick winds.

Chris Green

Chapter 4

The streetlights were gleaming down on top of Ryan's head as he walked from Faith's housed to the stash spot. He pushed it down 5th and Montgomery and made his way into the dark alley. After climbing the dirty fire escape to the vacant apartment, he opened the window to the third floor and quickly jumped inside. Entering the hallway, Ryan slid the solid piece of sheetrock to the side. He grabbed the duffle bag that rested behind it, slid the zipper back, and checked the spin barrel of his 357 Magnum. Ryan placed it on his hip along with a black Glock 40. He placed the bag back in its original spot, straightened the giant sheetrock, and exited the apartment.

Ryan climbed back out of the window, cleared the fire es-cape, and made his way out of the alleyway. He was sure not to be seen by any fiends. They were slick and wouldn't hesitate to double back on a nigga if you were slipping. He pulled out his cell and dialed DJ's line. After the second ring, it was picked up.

"What's good, bro?"

"Shit. I'm ready for the action. I took care of that," Ryan re-plied.

"Bet. Meet us on 4th and Adams. We already out here."

"On the way." He hung up.

* * *

After spotting the crew huddled up in Cheek Raw's blue Crown Vic, he made his way across to the dead end and got inside the car.

Wasting no time, he cranked the car and began to explain the mission. By the time they were in Browntown, it was already set. After sliding down on Anchorage Street, Ryan and DJ hopped out.

"Listen, all y'all gotta do is wait for the signal," Cheek stated before he got out of the car.

"That's all good. Just be on point 'cause I don't wanna have to bust this bitch," Ryan warned as they moved towards the dark spot of the street.

Not only was DJ Ryan's best friend, but they had been laying niggas down since they were thirteen. It was all money to them.

Sitting on the back of his Crown Vic, Cheeks called their victim's phone.

"Yo?"

"Wassup, Dee. It's me. I'm sitting outside the spot, nigga."

"Why you ain't tell me you was stopping through? What's good?" he asked.

"Yeah, but I needed to speak some business with you. I just happened to be in the area."

"Cool. I'll be out in a second."

Standing in the shadows, Ryan tensed up as he spotted the mark coming out of his home. He was a short, dark-skinned man with a beer belly. His appearance was exactly how Cheek Raw explained to them earlier that day. Ryan watched him step off the porch. He moved towards Cheeks and embraced him in a hug.

"You ready?" He nudged DJ.

"Go, nigga."

Moving towards the car, they crept up extra smoothly without being noticed. Before he could peep the movement, Ryan was up in his grill with the .357. "Don't move, fuck nigga!"

DJ wasted no time running his pockets to remove the paper he carried. "Damn, Cheeks. It's like that?" Dee's hands shook like Beyoncé's on the "Single Ladies" video.

"Hell yeah it's like that, pussy. I don't fuck with you, old head."

"Where the cake at? You got some more in the house, don't you?" Ryan wasn't letting up easy. The pistol was pressed against his mouth and he knew at any moment that bitch would explode.

"My family in there, young bull. It's all sitting on the living room table."

"Y'all niggas wait here. I'll be back."

Pushing him towards the house, Ryan held then gun closer to him before they entered the living room. A pound of marijuana and a bundle of money sat neatly on the coffee table. It looked as if Dee got stopped in the middle of his counting session. The lights were off in the home and the flat screen TV was the only thing giving him some room to see.

"Sit yo' bitch ass on the couch." Ryan punched him square in the eye.

Grabbing the dead presidents off the table, he began to stuff it all in his pockets. There was so much cash he began to stuff it inside his pants. He picked up the bag of weed and waved the strap. "Who all in the back?"

"My baby mama and kids. I swear, young bull." He sweated profusely.

"So if I trash yo' shit, I won't find no naked bitches in the back bagging up, correct?"

"No. There's nothing else. I'm just getting by. It's nothing else for me to give, li'l bro." His reply sounded like more of a plea instead of a man standing up for his honor.

Twirling the gun with a smirk, he accidently pulled the trig-ger, sending a bullet in the air. The shot startled Ryan, causing him to look down at the revolver. His heartbeat had sped up a pace and his ears were lightly ringing. The sounds of shuffling could be heard in the back of his home and the sight of Dee's slumped body sent anger through his body.

"Shit!" He panicked before bailing out of the home. Cheeks and DJ could sense the tragic look on his face as he ran back towards the car.

"What the fuck happened? I heard a gunshot," DJ asked.

"Let's go! We gotta get the fuck out of here." He wasted no time jumping into the Crown Victoria.

"I can't take y'all on nothing else," Cheek Raw said with a blowed expression before smashing off.

* * *

3 a.m., Ryan's bedroom

After splitting the couple grand three ways, Ryan listened to Cheek Raw talk about how stupid he was for murdering a peon. He wasn't even about that life, which meant that a gun didn't need to be used in the process. Instead of sticking around to listen, he made his way back to the crib for a piece of mind.

After making it home, he replayed Cheek's question back through his mind. "What did you kill 'im for, bro. That's a free body for nothing."

Ryan's only reply was, "He bucked."

Of course after locking up his bedroom, Ryan removed all the money from his pockets and added to the funds. What looked like a little turned out to be $35,000 on the head. Placing that with the six grand he snatched earlier, he grossed a cool $40,000 within twenty-four hours. It was never his intentions to keep the money on the hush and slime the boys, but the questioning of why he killed Dee had him puzzled. It was the rules to accept death as it comes in the streets. They were so worried about the murder being on their hands that they couldn't even tell them about the ass of cash he stuffed inside of his pockets. Neither could he spit out that the murder was an accident. He never intended to kill Dee. The freak accident spooked him also, but the matter of life and death wasn't on his hands. Only God.

* * *

5th and Monroe. DJs crib, 6:54 a.m.

"Darius! Darius! Get up. You're gonna be late for school boy. You ain't got nothing but a few months left," his mom screamed, waking him out of his sleep

"Oh shit!" he mumbled, still tired from the caper they pulled yesterday.

Getting out of bed, DJ stretched and yawned. After prepping himself for school, he thought back to the previous night. He didn't feel like he had killed anyone and he wasn't shook a bit. He didn't even lose any sleep. It surely wasn't haunting him like he thought it would.

He dressed in a red and black Champion sweater and put on a crisp pair of Zara jeans, placing a pair of red and black shell toe Adidas on his feet. He headed for the door. Arriving at Newark High, DJ looked at every face that passed by him in the thick hallway. It seemed like everyone knew their dirty secret. No one moved about loud and laid back as usual. It was more timid today for some reason.

As Nyla and Cheyenne approached him with a hug apiece, he snapped out of his paranoia state.

"Hey, best friend," Nyla greeted him first.

"Wassup, girl? What's good, Cheyenne?" He play punched her shoulder.

"Nothing. Wassup with yo' bad-ass brother? Ryan in the twelfth grade and still don't come to school?" Cheyenne asked.

"I don't know. He doin' him, I guess. Where the hell is Rose?" he questioned with his eyes roaming around the hallway.

"She over by Ms. Henderson's class with Faith. I gotta get to class, boy. See you after school."

Watching the girls walk off, he headed for the next hallway. Turning the corner, DJ spotted Faith and Rose from a distance. Rose was looking too good to be true. Her blonde weave hung down to her back and her precious baby-skinned face reminded you of a young Kimora Lee Simmons. Rose was a bad one. Even though she had a head full of natural hair and a natural body. She just chose to be ghetto. She was black, if you let her tell it. She was thick with curves like a baseball. She and Faith wore the same pink Northface jacket, skintight jeans, and Ugg boots.

When DJ approached the girls, he stared down at Rose's 5'4" frame.

"Hey, baby." She smiled, embracing him with a light kiss.

"What's good with you?" He nibbled on her cheek.

"Hey, brother," Faith acknowledged him.

"Wassup, sis?" Turning his attention back to Rose, he stepped closer. "Why you ain't come through my house yesterday?"

"Uh uh. Stop it. Boy, you was out with Ryan all day. Don't act all sweet and concerned now." She laughed.

"That don't mean I wouldn't have left his ass for you. Real talk." DJ ran his usual game.

"Nah. You would rather be with ya homie."

"Speaking of Ryan, his ass was supposed to call me last night. Where the hell were y'all?" Faith asked with a hand on her hip.

"First of all, I wasn't even with... Hold up! What y'all got go-ing with the interrogation process? Y'all sound worse than my mom. And we weren't with no other bitches."

"Girl, don't it sound like he lying?" Rose said with a smirk.

"Sure does," Faith added.

"Ha ha ha. Very funny, Miss Know It All. How about we make it up to y'all tonight?"

"Umm. How you suppose y'all gon' do that?"

"We can go catch some dinner and do a little shop-ping," DJ said, flipping his collar.

"No. Dinner is okay, but I refused to let Ryan spend any of that blood money on me. If I do that, it's like I'm glorifying it to be right and it's not." Faith crossed her arms.

"Not really. Let that man take care of you, girl. You know it's hard for us to run across this bread on a regular unless it's being in the streets. Ryan is gonna be that way forever."

"And he'll be that way forever by himself. I'm not with it."

"I feel you, sis. Y'all just get to class and we will see about it when we leave," DJ said, giving Rose a smooch to the cheek.

"A'ight. Oh yeah, Wicked and Reckless were looking for you. They claimed it was important," Faith warned him before walking off with Rose.

"Bet."

Turning towards the south side of the twelfth grade hallway, he made his way to his brother's section of the school. He stopped at his locker and opened it up to retrieve his binder. The yellow and blue folder rested on top of his bottom shelf. As he reached for them, a slight pinch pierced his neck. He turned around to see Wicked and Reckless in his personal space. He mushed them both.

"Y'all niggas know I'm extra 'noid. What the hell y'all got going?"

"Nothing much. Just bouncing around the school, looking for you and Ryan's ass," Reckless said. "I heard y'all niggas out here eating real good. Let me hold something."

"Shh! Damn, nigga. Don't alert everybody. Me and Ryan busted a li'l move yesterday for about six G's a piece. Keep that on the low." DJ smiled.

"Six? Y'all niggas definitely cutting the check today. Put us on and quit playing." Wicked smiled with excitement.

"Don't do that. You know we gon' spread the love. We gotta move lightly though. Last night some shit went down that we don't need being exposed."

"Man, you know that whatever is said within this circle is gonna stay with us. Don't act like we be on the running tongue shit, bro. We boys." Reckless nudged him in the chest playfully.

"Facts, my guy. I don't know what the hell Ryan got going on. I ain't heard from him since we split last night. He didn't even show up for school."

"That's Ryan for ya. I'm talking about Cheeks though. I know he putting y'all in position. Tell that nigga we want in. It's enough money for the killers to get some too. Not just the rob-bers," Reckless said with a serious face.

His mind was surely on the grind more for him and his cousin. There was no way that they were landing a body count from Arizona to Delaware and dues weren't being given. It was the known part of the game. Keep the shootas on a leash with the paper and everyone would make it home safely for dinner.

"Cheek is definitely putting shit in motion. All you need is patience. He already knows y'all ready, so that's the good part. We supposed to be meeting up with this nigga after school, so y'all need to be on point. Besides that, just relax," DJ assured him.

"Enough said." Wicked gave him some dap just as the bell rang.

"I'll catch y'all later." He headed straight for his homeroom class.

Chapter 5

Stepping into the prison facility, Kimyetta headed straight for the front desk. "Excuse me, sir. My husband was shipped to Georgia a few weeks back. I'm here to grab his property and my video visit that was set up, if possible. I know that I should be able to still view him because his inmate number wouldn't change."

"ID please," the voice of the intake clerk demanded.

"Excuse me?"

"Your ID," he repeated. The top of his head was sweating heavily and obviously he had an attitude.

If the places were different, Kimyetta would've probably spit in his face for his disrespectful-ass energy. Instead of biting his bait, she held her tongue. Kimyetta didn't need anything stop-ping her from getting Raekwon's property from the prison.

"Whose property are you here to pick up?" he asked while looking at her identification card.

"Raekwon Royal. I also have a visit with him over the kiosk. He's being held in Georgia, so I paid for my thirty minutes yesterday."

"I heard you the first time, ma'am. I'm just making sure all of this adds up and you can be on about your way."

Taking a deep breath, Kimyetta thought about rocking his ass with her own shank. It subsided when he handed her the ID back.

"Go ahead down to the main intake. You can pick up the property and have your visit. His time has already started, so you might want to hurry." He flashed a crooked-ass buttery smile.

"Thanks, bitch," she spat before heading through the next metal door.

After picking up Raekwon's belongings, she stuffed it inside of a plastic bag and headed for the visitation computers. Sitting down, she scrolled on the screen until she found his name. She clicked the video visit and his face appeared on the screen minutes later. She couldn't help but to smile.

"What's up, Kim? It took yo' ass long enough. I thought that we would have to pay for another visit." He held the phone tightly to his ear.

"Nigga, shut up. I ain't never failed yo' ass before. Good times or bad. You're Raekwon Royal. I'm always here. Don't try me, boy," she shot back.

Laughing, he flapped the collar of his white state shirt. "Sorry for moving so much. It's hot as fuck down here in Georgia. I don't know how long they trying to keep me down here. After this trial, I'll be shipped back to Delaware for the next case."

"That's good. Hopefully they will drop that bullshit and send you back soon. We need you out here, Raekwon." Her voice trailed off as she played with her nails to shake the sadness.

"I know. How's Ryan?"

"Ryan's ass is two seconds from me blowing his damn head off. He ain't going to school and all his mind want to do is follow in your steps. He has totally lost it, Raekwon."

"What? I mean, I knew his school shit was a little rocky. What he did now?"

"What he ain't did? He don't wanna bring his ass in the house and I keep going through bullshit with his school and the police. He's dangerous, and everybody is out there scared of him, Kwon. I know that he's your son, but something has to stop. He really smelling himself, and that ain't even the half. I've called to the school just to check on him and it's the fourth time. They told me that he wasn't present. This is his last year, Raekwon. He needs to graduate." Kimyetta blew out a deep breath in frustration.

"I feel you on that, Kim. I really do. But Ryan ain't gonna lis-ten to neither one of us, ma. That's just the real side of it. I know it may be hard to accept, but I went through the same thing at his age. I know that I should be with him around this time and it's eating him up. I don't know what the judge is gonna do about this case. If things go sour, I'm not only gonna lose you or my baby boy. Listen, Kimyetta, you have to stop being so hard on him. He's holding that anger, and it's coming from the pressure with you."

"Raekwon, I've tried that with Ryan's grown ass. He takes my kindness for weakness. I had to throw a frying pan at his ass in order for him to listen the other day. Regardless of if I yell or not, he doesn't have the right to disobey his mother. He can leave first," she stated with authority.

"That's understood, but as I said, he's gonna be rebellious if you continue to do that. My momma did the same shit and I bottled it all up until I finally exploded. It hurt to admit that I didn't want to be like the other kids. But her aggravation pushed it out of me even more. He don't listen to shit you say because you're yelling and cursing in the mix of grilling him. All you gotta do is talk, baby. He'll slow down; trust me."

"I hear you, Raekwon."

"Look, my time is almost up. Tell Ryan I love him and I love you also. Soon this shit will be over, so I need to get everybody prepared."

"Stop saying that shit!" Kimyetta snapped.

"It's just the truth. Stop trying to deny it. We always been re-al and we ain't finna stop now. Let that boy know that this path is not what he wants. Either he wants life to be free, or he wants a cell for the rest of his natural born life, " he said with serious-ness in his posture.

"I hear you. We love you too, Kwon."

"A'ight. Whatever happens at the trial, you'll be the first to know." He blew her a kiss through the screen.

Kimyetta returned his gesture. She hung up the phone.

The last few seconds of that video call sent so many memo-ries through Kim's mind. It was hard to see her love behind the wall facing so much pain. It could be the last time she ever got to see her man in the streets again. She only wished that she could stay a little while longer. It was a long ride back home, and nothing could take her mind away from Raekwon's last words. "My time is almost over with." It was a sentence that would eat at her until they freed hi, she thought before walking out of the building.

* * *

After making it back home to her safe haven, Kimyetta quickly showered and caught the next episode of her TV show. Lying on the couch, she pondered Raekwon's advice about their son. There was a time where she used to show him so much compassion, love that only a mommy could show. She did began to yell a lot after his incarceration. There was never the thought of him feeling down about his dad because she was too torn about his bid to understand. Her child was suffering too. It made him into the animal that she didn't want to see.

She got up to straighten her home, grabbing the broom. It was probably the only thing she could do to get the non-sense off of her mind. She picked up Ryan's jacket and headed for his room. She opened up his closet door and reached for a hanger to place it on the rack. There was a huge black bag that caught her eye. She used her foot to slide it over. She felt the heaviness and won-dered what could be inside. It was never seen in her house be-fore, and that was all the rights to run through that shit.

She unzipped it, reached in, and pulled out ten thousand dol-lars. It was all tied together with at least three rubber bands. The small specks of blood on the bills caused her to drop it on the floor. Here she was struggling with SSI checks and a regular nine to five and this boy had two years of rent inside of his closet. There was no telling where he got the devil paper from. It surely wasn't earned the correct way.

Digging back through the duffle, she touched some-thing hard inside of an inside pocket. She reached in and removed the two handguns and shook her head. It was re-ally official. Her son was fully connected to the streets, and he was becoming an addict for trouble. It was Raekwon's idea to talk, but that was now out of the window. All she wanted him to do was pack his shit and get the hell out before she watched him make the same mistakes as his fa-ther. She was going to let him crumble on the turf by him-self. There was nothing sadder than being a bad parent. It never happened on Kim's watch before and it wasn't about to start now. The only thing she had to prepare her son for was the real world, because he was about to finally get his taste of it.

* * *

Raekwon, Reidsville state prison, 1:20 p.m.

After making his way from the chow hall, Raekwon stepped through his dorm's front door. It was a drain session hearing about Ryan and Kimyetta's problems. Bad enough that he wasn't able to provide their usual way of life. But now his son was about to be a product of his environment also. Still and all, no matter what he felt, things would only get better if it was meant. It was God's natural way of pain or happiness. Life or death. Even love and hate. It was decreed to be the way it would.

He walked into his room and opened his locker to retrieve his things for the shower. As he roamed inside of the box, four men stepped through the door with their weapons drawn.

"You know what this is, Raekwon," a huge bald dude spoke with aggression.

He took his head out of the box and stared at the men with a smirk. "Oh shit. So I guess this is the moment where I'm sup-posed to ask for y'all to spare me, huh?"

"Cut the tough guy shit, dawg. You can save all that for your meeting with God," the man replied while his other goons stood with unmerciful faces.

Moving swifter than a cat, Raekwon punched one of the men square in his shit, watching him fall to the floor. He shot a bow towards his next attacker.

The room was only so big, and all the muscle that was in the mix made it hard for everyone to attack Raekwon the right way.

A sharp blow to his neck sent him down to the floor in pain. The rest of the men wasted no time restraining him for better access.

"I like ya style, Raekwon. But you know how this shit goes. You take ours. We take you." The bald man spat, sending a glob of spit into his face.

Raekwon began to catch his breath. "Nigga, I invented this shit. Ain't no such thing as explaining nothing. You Gangsta, right?" he challenged. It was the same way he tested Solo.

"True indeed."

Cutting the conversation short, the man quickly plunged the knife into the side of Raekwon's neck, holding him so that he couldn't jump around. The lead G.D. repeatedly pumped the steel through his face and neck, hitting him a few times on the stom-ach. The men let him collapse to the floor.

"Make sure y'all remember my name, nigga!" Raekwon spat as blood poured severely from his mouth and wounds.

The cold grasp of death came closer, causing his legs to go numb. Before he could feel the last breath escape his body, he smiled, knowing that his life mission would be the one the one to would be accomplished. He was the true monster of Delaware, and it would be that way until his son rose to the top.

Chris Green

Chapter 6

Ryan, 7th and Madison

Leaving Faith's best friend Demerea's house, Ryan made his way towards the house, hoping to beat the clock. He thought about his mom being on the bullshit, especially when she made the comment about him missing school. He knew that she was still having her visit today with his father along with a hair ap-pointment. It left just enough room for him to get down on class without Kimyetta being alert. He prayed that she didn't have a reason to start snooping. He needed to get home and remove the duffle bag from his closet.

As he reached 5th Street, he placed on his bookbag to blend in with the Newark high schoolers. He spotted Faith, DJ, Wick-ed, and Reckless. A bright smile came across his face.

"Yo!" Ryan called out before hugging Faith and dapping up his crew. "What's good with y'all?"

"Shit, you know, just going to school. Unlike some of you niggas," DJ laughed.

"Fuck y'all. What's the move doe?" He hugged Faith before she walked off to head home.

"I hear you and DJ making moves. Let a nigga eat," Reckless asked with his arms folded.

"Who you hear that from?" Ryan looked over to DJ. "Man, you know we a team. Don't do that. We ain't on no secret shit."

DJ shrugged his shoulders at Ryan "What else was I sup-posed to do?"

"That's cool and all, but I was gonna add y'all in when shit was ready. We don't need no pillow talking or random conversa-tions about what we doing. That goes for all y'all."

"Understood. Now how we gon' handle this business? Me and Wicked eating off scraps and I'm not with that," Reckless tried to press Ryan.

"That's all handled, bro. By tomorrow, we all will have some dough in our pocket."

"Exactly," DJ butted in. "Not just that, Cheek Raw hit me up this morning about us linking in with them bitches. I ain't never seen no females with the fuckery, so that might be a plus for us."

"Bitches on our team? Fuck no! Who the hell thought of that shit?" Ryan spit out his gum.

"Cheeks. He told me those Philly bitches put in work, and they thorough."

"I don't care how thorough they is. At the end of the day, a bitch still got the potential to be a rat. I already don't trust niggas, so why would I trust a bitch?" Ryan stated.

"So you don't trust me, nigga?" DJ air-boxed towards his face.

"That ain't no question. You're my best friend. We've been knowing each either since we were seven. That doesn't even stand for you."

"Then trust me now, nigga. I did my homework on these hoes. They copping more work than hustlas out of Delaware, and them bitches laying down licks like they took a college course for the shit," DJ assured them.

Not liking the idea, Ryan held his opinions and decided that he was going to see how it went.

"Plus, I wanna see what these hoes got to offer. And I'm def-initely interested in these bands, not the bitches," DJ added.

"How much money these hoes talking?" Wicked asked.

"20 to 30 thousand. That's not including what all we can grab in dope. That's why we're having a meeting, to see what these folks talking about. We ain't got nothing but a cool hour to be there."

"A'ight, bet. Let me get dressed and I'll meet y'all down there."

Ryan dapped up all three of his boys.

Ryan walked down the street and entered the corner store. After buying a bag of chips and a Brisk soda, he headed for the house. He slid up his stairs, entered the apartment, and headed straight for the refrigerator. After placing his drink in the freezer, he headed upstairs. When he opened his bedroom door, his eyes landed on Kimyetta with all the blood money on her lap.

"Where the fuck did this shit come from?" Her eyes were beaming down on him.

He could see the hurt written on her face, but it was a solid fact that the street had ahold of Ryan. He began to worry even more when she pulled the guns from behind her.

"Ma, it's not even mines. I was about to return it."

"Bitch, you got guns in my fucking house. I gave you every-thing yo' ass asked me for. I told you time after time about your stupid behavior, Ryan. This is insane. You car-rying around weap-ons now?"

All he could do was stand there with a clueless face. He hon-estly didn't know what to say.

"Ms. Reynolds, your schoolteacher, told me that a stu-dent's mother called her about you shooting at him. The entire hood knows what you're doing around here because you don't know how to listen and stay out of the way. I tried to be patient. I tried to let you breeze away, hoping that you would change. I see now that I wasted my time."

"Mama, them folks lying. I've never shot at nobody. I'm try-ing, but this shit just ain't for me. I wanna make sure we don't need for anything, and you can't do that right now. I'm tired of living like this. My dad is a street legend. I'm not going out bad. I just want some money." Ryan folded his arms with an angry frown.

"Your father was a renegade. He cared about nothing but the streets, which left his ass hanging in the end. He wasn't smart. You wanna know why, Ryan? Because he didn't give a fuck. Just like you. How can your heart say that you care for me if you won't even listen, boy? If I get a call about your body being found, that shit would crush me. Nothing matters more to me than my damn son. You're seventeen, not twenty-nine. Did you hurt anyone to get this money and guns? Don't fucking lie to me," she warned, raising her hand before he spoke.

"Ma, I made my own way out there, and you know I'm not going to lie to you. I took a nigga off for the money because we needed it. In the mix of that, he was shot. And yes, he died. I didn't mean for it to happen, but it just happened. How else can we survive if we don't have a way to eat, ma?" Ryan sat on the bed next to her.

Shaking her head, Kimyetta wiped the small tear from her eye. "I never meant for you to turn out this way. All I wanted was to take care of you and teach the way of a nor-mal family." She rose to her feet and gazed into his eyes. "I love you, but I refuse to see my own child kill himself. I want you out of my house by nine tonight. And there's no exceptions."

"Ma." He stood up as she headed for the door.

Ignoring his call, she slammed the door behind her.

Ryan slumped down on the bed. He thought about Faith and the new seed that was coming. He never even had a chance to tell Kimyetta that she was about to be a grand-mother. The choice for the street life chose him. He was destined to be a hustler, and it wasn't gonna stop just because his mama felt that it wasn't cool.

Packing up his bags and weapons, he left from his room and made his way out of the front door.

* * *

DJ, Cheek Raw's spot, 5th and Monroe.

"We need to be on top of our shit if we really about to do this," Cheek said as everybody sat around his living room.

"Exactly .If we moving it, has to be official 'cause I ain't going down for no bullshit," DJ spoke up.

Staring at the faces around the table, Ryan did a runback of what everybody said. Off top, he was digging the chick Sekoya. Her brown caramel complexion was booming, and her dress game was impeccable. She was the only one stressing loyalty over everything, even the paper. Her bright yellow nails would fly up when she was speaking on some real shit. It was a natural blessing in her eyes to get paper together. Her style was the most valuable out of all three girls, but that was something the guys could spot from a mile away.

The next was Teona, who was mostly a good girl gone bad. By the way she spoke, nothing was going to be trusted in any-one's mind when it came to her. Her small head sported a low hairstyle. Her skinny body was smaller than Wiz Khalifa, and the fake grill in her mouth gleamed like she pulled it straight out of a Maxway ring box. You could tell by her accent that she was suburb raised. She definitely was holding a little paper, judging from the grey Mercedes Benz C class she arrived in earlier. The worst thing on the streets was an imposter, and she was surely the first candidate. The only thing she would be able to do for every-one was get them killed. She wasn't built for the missions that were ahead, and no one could tell Ryan any different.

The third was a bit different. Tyleema barely said a word. She mostly nodded at everything that was said and continued to ask when the show was beginning. The only time she opened her mouth was to correct Cheeks on something. She was offended about the introduction from him. Comparing her to a worker caused shit to get a little steamy in the home, especially when she claimed to pop her gun harder than any nigga in the room. She was heated, but eventually calmed her nerves and tossed the situation to the side as if it never happened. Ryan could also tell that DJ was smelling a little lust for her by the way he stared.

After meeting the women, Ryan was ready to get involved with the dangerous festivities. From the looks of things, DJ was right. The movement with the chicks would only broaden their vision. The ability to get closer to a nigga was a trick for a bitch specifically. If the caper went smoothly, the Rich and Royal movement would take Delaware by surprise. Wicked and Reck-less didn't say much, but that was clearly a sign that they were ready also.

After discussing the business, everyone seemed to linger around, so Ryan decided to make his move before it got late.

"Yo, Cheek. Let me holla at you in the back, big bro."

Spotting the look on Ryan's face, he abandoned the company and followed him into the room.

"What's good, li'l bro? You look stressed."

"Man, my fucking mama kicked me out."

"What? Kim kicked you out? Get the fuck on. You lying," he replied in disbelief.

"Nah, I'm serious. I ain't got no fucking where to go. I'ma need to crash at yo' spot for a little bit, bro." Ryan frowned.

Cheek sat back, thinking for a second. Cheek snapped his finger. "Look. I got a spot out on 8th and Adams. It's a duck off, so I don't need my shit to get hot. I can give you the keys and let you crash there until shit gets right for you. It's already decked out so you don't need nothing like that. Just take care of my shit, Ryan." Cheek looked at him seriously.

"You know I got you, bro."

"I can't tell, nigga. You smiling too hard. I'm dead-ass seri-ous, Ryan. Take care of my shit," he ordered before tossing him the keys.

"I said I got ya, nigga. Calm down. You know I'ma make it back up to ya, nigga." He smirked before walking out of the room.

Getting back to the front room, Ryan took his place at the roundtable. "So have we came up on anything?"

"Facts. I told them about the li'l move for that other thirty piece. It's a quick check and easy enough for us to finesse that," DJ said.

"And just like I told you, we all can't split thirty bands. We might as well just rob the Family Dollar down the street." Sekoya crossed her legs.

Everybody laughed in unison.

"What makes you so sure on what we can do? You must got something lined up that's better for us?" Ryan asked with a straight face.

Looking him up and down, she giggled. "Of course I do. I wouldn't have opened my mouth if I didn't."

"I'm waiting."

She shrugged her shoulders at his pushiness. She scooted closer to the table. "First off, my move is clean and easy. Two guys move around this home to protect one fuck man. He eats the real way. Dope, cars, whatever. I know for sure that he getting forty thousand a week. That's on a bad week. He always ready to spend some bread on a bitch. Besides eating pussy on Saturdays, he doesn't move often, but he re-ups on Sunday, so the best time to come at his throat is the weekend."

"Where does he stay?" Ryan asked eagerly.

"Edgemore."

"That's a sweet-ass neighborhood. When do you say is best, Friday?"

"You're not listening. I told you he loves to eat pussy on Saturdays." Sekoya smiled. "But you know how niggas are. They let us know everything that we shouldn't know, and keep shit secretive that we should know. It's a part of the game."

Respecting her mouth piece, Ryan learned forward. "Since you speak so smooth, we gon' rock with this. I hope your robbing game is pretty like you, because I ain't into saving nobody." He winked his eye.

"No need, pretty boy. I can pop my own shit," she replied arrogantly.

"You got a few tricks, but I got a few too. So this how we gon' do this..."

***

The next two days went by like water floating down a drain. The mission was in effect and Ryan was riding down the back street to their mark's home. Sekoya texted five minutes prior to tell the boys about the process. The back door was unlocked, and all they had to do was cater to the two dick riders in the base-ment. The rest would be a cake walk.

Arriving at the spot, Ryan stepped out of his car with DJ, Reckless, and Wicked by his side. Of course Teona and Tyleema occupied their fake security guards, but it was never wrong to be on point.

Sliding quickly through the backyard the crew headed up the steps and entered the kitchen. The silent home was exquisite. There were obviously two floors - three, including the basement. The faint noise under their feet could be heard through the floor.

Waving his hand, Ryan signaled for Wicked and Reckless to head for the bottom floor company. He and DJ proceeded up the steps with their guns aimed. Sliding around to the master bed-room, they moved down the narrow hallway until reaching his door. As they crept inside, Sekoya slid out of his bed and grabbed ahold of her clothes. Moving towards the bed, Ryan stood over Tech, who snored lightly.

Whack! The handle of his gun crashed against his skull.

"Yo, what the fuck!" he screamed in pain. His clothes were scattered over the floor and his expensive jewelry was the only thing that he wore on his body.

"Shut the fuck up. Stop screaming or I'ma blow yo' shit off." Ryan mashed the gun through his teeth. "Let me see the cash or I'm wiping ya nose and killing shit in the pro-cess. Where it at, Tech?"

"Why the fuck you robbing me, bro? I don't even know you. Sekoya, what the fuck? I thought we had something?" He pan-icked as she zipped up her black Puma hoodie.

"You thought wrong, li'l daddy."

"Fuck all that. Cough it up, pussy. 5, 4, 3, 2…"

"Chill, nigga. The shit in my safe. Right hand side of the clos-et."

"Just watch him, bro. If he moves, kill his ass."

DJ walked over to the closet, snatching it open. He fol-lowed the directions and spotted the jackpot. He dropped down in front of the safe. He looked behind him. "What's the fucking code?"

"1190," Tech stuttered.

Ryan and Sekoya glared at him with murderous eyes.

The sound of a nigga yelling could be heard beneath them. Seconds after, three gunshots released, tensing eve-rybody in the room.

"What the fuck's going on down there?" Sekoya looked at Ryan, confused.

"I don't fucking know. DJ, hurry up. We gotta go."

"Just relax. I'm coming," he replied while scraping the safe's earnings into a black garbage bag, making sure that he grabbed everything. DJ got up and slid out of the small space. "This ain't no hundred. I can bet you that."

"Fuck it. We just gotta leave it."

"No the fuck we ain't. It's more in here. That ain't it." Sekoya held Tech's pistol. "Where that other shit you showed me?"

"You dirty-ass bitch. Why are you doing this?" Tech fumed with sweat dropping down his nose.

"You playing a role and you got more shit stashed in this bitch." Ryan grabbed the pillow from behind his back, placing it on his leg. He fired the weapon, sending cotton flying loose.

"Muthaffffucka!" Tech bit his bottom lip in severe pain. The bullet tore straight through his leg.

"Next one is in the chest, dumbo." Ryan was ready to end the entire situation.

"I got a couple of keys in the deep freezer downstairs. Just take it." He landed heavily.

"It's time to fucking go, bro," DJ pressed while glancing at his watch.

"I'm ready." Ryan sent a shot through Tech's heart.

Boom!

The gun smoked lightly before they all turned to leave the room, moving swiftly back through the hallway. They bumped into Wicked coming up the steps.

"We got a problem, Ryan."

"What happened? I could hear all that shit from upstairs?"

They headed down to living room. The sight of a bloody man lying on the floor caused Sekoya to turn her head. Teona and Tyleema held guns with their hoodies tied tight. Reckless walked back and forth with his gun aimed at another nigga in front of him. He was sitting on the floor with blood leaking from his mouth.

"DJ, hit the kitchen and grab that," Ryan mumbled in his ear. He moved over to the injured man, who breathed awkwardly. He glanced down at the wallet by his hand, turning open the pouch. He stared at the ATF badge, then glanced up into the man's eyes. He slowly stood up and backed away.

"How did this happen?" he asked Reckless.

"He whipped out this pussy-ass gun, trying to be a general. I had to!" Reckless yelled with tension in his body.

"Nigga, calm the fuck down. We don't need to make this shit louder than it already is. We leaving now." Ryan looked over to Sekoya as DJ returned from the kitchen.

"What about him, Ry?" she asked.

The man couldn't move or speak, but his eyes scanned all of them as he breathed erratically.

Contemplating on what to do, Ryan shook his head. There was no other choice. He raised the gun to his face. The man slowly lifted his hand in front of him. The sight of his bloody face flashed through Ryan's mind like a photo was being taken. It was never hard to pull the trigger, but something about this time just didn't seem right. Instead of following his first mind, he allowed the bullet to blow like a gust of hurricane wind. The shot landed in the center of the Agent's chest and he slumped over. The crew exited the front door, leaving their catastrophe behind.

Chapter 7

Faith; Demerea's house

"I ain't seen Ryan in like three days. The last time that we were around each other was when we went out to eat with Rose and DJ," Faith said as she lay back on Demerea's bed.

Besides watching a couple of movie, they gossiped about miscellaneous shit and brought up the conversation on cheating-ass dogs.

"How many times have I have to tell you that Ryan is bad news? You already knew that when you caught him fucking the little red bitch from up top. It's destined for him to be a slimy-ass dog," Demerea said with hatred.

"I don't hold grudges."

"Bitch, you sprung."

"No I'm not." Faith laughed.

"Seriously. You being treated like some second brand of ce-real while this boy has his way. That's crazy! If I was you, I would talk to Keem. He's a cool-ass nigga and he has major respect." Demerea flicked through channels on her television.

"Keem? That nigga in the streets just like Ryan. And you know they know each other. That's stupid. I'm not just no bounce around girl. I got enough on my hands already. Ryan would try to kill me." Faith frowned. "Keem is just my homie. Nothing more. Nothing less. All we do is study together."

"Yeah right. Y'all probably already smacking buns on the low,
bitch." Demerea snickered.

"I love Ryan. Fuck every other nigga. I'm not worried about no damn Keem. Unfortunately, one man has my heart and that ain't changing for nothing."

"Alright. Let Keem slide his pretty little ass my way. Fuck around and put that pussy on his ass." Demerea grinded on Faith's arm with a freaky smile.

"Bitch, you crazy!"

Demerea was known to act a fool and she was always ten toes down about her friends and family. Her medium build was just enough weight to toss hoes around with ease. Even though she hadn't grown up to be successful like the rest of her older brothers and sisters, she maintained her own, and that was all that counted. She truly warned Faith about Ryan's actions, but time after time, Faith let it breeze past her. It even came down to a certain time where she wanted to confront him in front of Faith. It was still re-jected. In the end, her conversation today made a valuable point. If Ryan couldn't respect the love she had for him, how were they gonna co-parent for their child?

"I'm telling you, Faith. You could have any one you want. Bitch, you fine as hell!"

"I know, I know. I'm just gon' see if shit gets better. Speak-ing of him, I need to call and see if I can get an an-swer."

Pulling out her cell, she dialed Ryan's number, tapping her finger lightly on Demerea's bed. His voice spoke through the line.

"Yeah?"

"Where have you been? I've called you a hundred times these past few days," she snapped.

"I've been home, Faith."

"Yeah, right. That sounds like a lie."

"I don't give a fuck what you think. I just told you that I been at home. I ain't got time for none of that bitch-ass shit," Ryan spat with anger in his tone.

'Who are you talking to like that? What's wrong with you?

"My dad died. I don't feel like even being bothered right now, Faith. It's just not the right time." He hung up in her ear.

Staring at the phone, she covered her mouth. "Oh my God."

"Bitch, what? That nigga better not be calling you out yo'

name." Demerea walked over to her.

"No, it's his dad."

"Raekwon? What, did he get the death penalty?"

"He's dead."

* * *

Kimyetta, 614 W. 5th Street

After Kim received the news of Raekwon's death earlier that morning, she decided enough was enough. The streets had al-ready claimed the lives of too many loved ones. Raekwon wasn't just a piece of the family. He was attached to her soul. His speech and spirit kept her pushing through all the hard times. All she had left was Ryan. Before she sat back and watched the last piece of her blood die by the polluted streets of terror, she made up her mind to escape Delaware for good. She packed all her important shit and clothes. She headed out of the door and climbed in the car. The only thing that was left for her to do was live her dream.

Ryan, new apartment, 8th and Adams

Ryan opened his eyes from thinking about everything his fa-ther told him before his death. The pain he felt was indescribable. The man who gave him life was taken away by the same game he controlled in his head. It was hard to accept him leaving, but Ryan knew that it came with the life. Death was only a day that you couldn't escape, no matter how hard you tried. Ryan didn't have it in him to drop a tear. Loyalty wasn't meant for man, only God. It was the only reason he didn't have any trust.

Downing a swig of his hot brown liquor, he rose to his feet.

All he could do was look around the quiet apartment. He didn't want to be bothered with anyone, but the memorial for his pops kept eating at his mind. He threw on his Nike sweater, slid into his boots, and headed out of the door.

Walking down towards 8th and Monroe, he spotted a dude named Killa posted in front of the liquor store.

"Hey Ryan. Can I holla at you for a minute, young bull?" he asked with sincerity.

Even though he didn't want to communicate too much, Killa had been one of Raekwon's personal associates before he spazzed out on crack. Respect still had to be shown. Ryan moved over to him. They embraced with a pound.

"Wassup, old head?"

"Look, I know that I ain't got much, but yo' daddy was like my brother, kid. You know whenever you need old Uncle Killa, I'll be here."

"Thanks," Ryan replied before walking off.

He made it around to 5th and Madison. The block moved around, grieving over Raekwon's demise. Not only did the death hit everyone's heart, but it left a gap in the streets. There would never be another Raekwon Royal.

The music from the loud stereo played. "I Miss You" by Aaliyah as everyone stood around the memorial shedding tears. Some people were happy and felt that Raekwon was a blessing for the hood, like it was a time to honor his name and rejoice instead of being sad. He held the hood intact and now they could pay their respects by making his name live on.

Ryan linked up with Wicked, DJ, and Reckless, who sat on the curb of 5th and Washington.

"Ryan, wassup, bro, you a'ight? I mean, I know you ain't, but - " "I'm good, DJ," he responded, not wanting to bring up his dad anymore.

"Yeah. You know we all brothers. Ain't no way you can't be here for ya dog when some shit like this going on. Kwon was like a father figure to us," Wicked added.

Ryan couldn't help but to sit and talk with his friends about old times and fun memories. After a while, it even started to cheer him up. The only reason it was so depressing was because his team had more memorable moments with his father than he did. Still and all, the feeling of the hood partying in the name of his dad kept the smile burning.

"We gon' be good, bro. Watch." DJ tapped Ryan's shoulder.

"Real shit, Ry, we gon' eat. Live it up for Raekwon!" Reck-less shouted.

"I am. Not only that, since a nigga playing foul, nobody can eat over here anymore without our permission. We ain't even leaving these bitch-ass niggas a crumb. We said that it's Rich and Royal over everything. That means this city. If it' not us, we have no mercy. And that's on my pops," Ryan promised with a hand over his heart.

"Real shit." DJ nodded.

"I feel y'all on that, but what we got lined up for this Rich and Royal movement? We touched a sixty and split that shit. This ain't gonna be enough for all of us to eat the real way."

"That depends on who sets up the move. We only doing this right now because we gotta build for what's to come. Today we could be eating a few grand, but tomorrow, we could have two hundred thousand. It's all about the respect and patience," Ryan confirmed.

"Word," Reckless agreed.

Deciding to abandon the block gathering, the boys headed back towards Madison.

"I can't afford not to eat. Faith is pregnant, and we ain't about to go out bad with our seed for no one. This is my time, and nobody getting in my way from us getting this money."

"Wait, Faith's pregnant?" DJ asked with a shocked ex-pres-sion.

"Yeah. I know it's shocking, it damn near tripped me out too. I'm not too good with handling bad news, but that just made things even more stressful. The time for getting money is now. Responsibilities need to be handled."

The boys' conversation was going okay until Killa re-appeared in front of him.

"Yo, Ryan. Let me get another second with you?" he asked. This time, his face wasn't so friendly.

"Wassup, old head? I just spoke to you the last time I passed. I really ain't got no kicking it right now."

"I know, but it's important."

Stepping to the side, Killa got close to Ryan so no one could hear their words.

"I just came down from 3rd. Talk around Delaware is that yo' dad got killed by some G.D. niggas. A few of them cats be down by the bridge, so I know that the gossip could easily lead to them. You don't wanna get flipped for not being on point," Killa said with folded arms.

"What? Who the fuck you hear some shit like that from?" Ryan was furious.

"Whoa, young bull. I ain't no snitch. I'm only doing this for the li'l love I shared with ya pops.

"Okay. I need you to tell them niggas something for me, old head." Ryan grabbed his shoulder.

"What's that, young bull?"

"This."

Boc! Ryan removed his gun and placed a slug into his brain.

As soon as the pistol released, people began to run in different directions. Wicked scattered down the street with Reckless directly behind him.

"Give me that shit, man!" DJ snatched the gun from Ryan. "Go!"

Snapping back into his body, Ryan realized that it was still daylight. Pacing off the street, he headed smoothly through the alleyway until he reached 8th and Adams, looking both ways before he crossed the street. He headed over to the spot.

After stepping inside, he placed his back against the door. The feeling of any badmouthing stressed him more than anything. Slandering the Royal family was against the code in his eyes. It was hard not to put the team in awkward predicaments. Things had to be done. Who better to do it than himself? It was respect 'til the death.

The sound of his phone ringing caused him to jump. Instead of answering, he stood in place to drain the nervousness from his system. Silence filled the air once his line stopped vibrating.

He took a seat on the couch and huffed. It wasn't even five minutes later before his cell began to sound off again. Snatching it from his pocket, he answered. "Yo, what's good!" his voice boomed.

"Don't yell at me. I know you're mad about your dad, but I am too. You can't take your pain out on everyone else, Ryan," Faith calmly spoke through the line.

"My bad, babe. I'm just trippin' out." He rubbed a hand across his curly hair.

"I know you are, but you have to calm down. We are gonna get through it together if you allow me. I'm only trying to be here for you, Ryan," she stressed through the receiver.

"I hear you."

"I walked to yo mom's house earlier to check up on you, and when I got to your street, she was leaving with a lot of bags. I asked her where you was, and she just looked at me. She said that she didn't know or care. Before I could say anything else, she got in the car and smashed out on me."

"What?

"Yes. What's going on, Ryan, and where are you at?"

"I got my own spot. Just come down on 8th and Adams," he replied before hanging up.

Chapter 8

Faith, 8th and Adams

Faith left Demerea's house as soon as she heard Ryan's whereabouts. She stood on the sidewalk watching cars drive past as she waited for him. Just as she was about to whip out her cell phone, Faith spotted him walking slowly out of an apartment building. It didn't take long before she closed their distance. She grabbed ahold of him. They rocked back and forth without speaking.

"Come on." Ryan pulled her towards the crib.

They moved briskly up the sidewalk. They entered his apart-ment and locked the doors behind them.

"Who spot is this?" Faith asked. She couldn't help but to glance at the clean furnishing and decor.

"Ours."

He led her straight to his bedroom and flopped down on the bed. Her body followed, sliding directly by his side. She couldn't help but to kiss his lips. The scary feeling of something happening to him worried her more than any-thing.

"How did you get it?" Faith asked curiously.

"My people threw me the keys .You know my mama kicked me out and shit. I ain't just down bad to the point where no one is in my corner. We gon' be here for about ten months and then we moving away from this shit.

"Your mom looked like she was leaving for good ear-lier." Faith raised up to look in his eyes.

"All I care about is you and my kid right now. My mama been plotting to do that. She was just not woman enough to do it sooner. I'm on my own. Get up and grab that bag out the corner." Ryan pointed.

Faith did as she was told, retrieving the bag. She walked back over to the bed and placed it in his hands.

Ryan showed her the giant rolls of cash. She gazed in amazement. "Ryan, where did this come from?"

"It don't matter because there's plenty more of it. Just know that our child is gonna have whatever by any means. I know you don't approve of the things I do, but without me doing this, you would have to start wondering if we're gonna be able to really do this. All you need to do is sit yo' ass back and birth my kid. It kills me every day that people will go here and work they ass off for chump change. I'm my own boss. My mom don't fuck with me. My dad is dead. And you pregnant. Fuck everyone that ain't me and you. I don't know why, but I'm just cold hearted, Faith. Everybody need you until they in a position to say fuck you. That won't be us."

Faith sat quietly as she listened to everything he said to her. It actually made perfect sense. Of course she felt obligated to respect his decision, but her opinion mattered too. Before Ryan found out that she was pregnant, his father was killed and his mother abandoned him. It was the reason for his anger. But Faith didn't want that to spiral out and lose everything they worked so hard for. She didn't want to stress him out anymore, so she played her part and decided to uplift her man.

"Alright, baby. I understand. And you do have something in your heart." She tapped the center of his chest. Don't say things like that. Demerea be ready to fight you, saying that you pos-sessed."

"Fuck that bitch. She don't know me." Ryan kissed Faith.

"Don't do my friend like that. You already got me. I don't care about the money, and I'm always gonna stand by your side. Right or wrong, I'm here through it all. I just want to motivate you. I been here before some cash. So never put that shit over me. I don't care how much it is," she warned.

"You right, but we need money to eat."

"I know you love money. But paper don't have feelings, Ryan. Even if it did, trust me, it damn sho' don't love you more than me. Now come here," Faith demanded

She laid on her back and pulled Ryan in between her legs. "I love you." Her whisper caressed his ear lightly.

"I love you too."

Sliding off her H & M jeans, he threw them to the side. He touched her pussy through the thin lace panties. He pushed his jeans to the floor, quickly rocking up. He licked his fingers to enhance her moistness. Feeling his fingers slip inside, he traded them with his manhood.

"Sss. Be easy, Ryan."

"I got you, baby. Just spread them legs wider," he ordered before sliding deeper.

"Oh shit," she whispered into the air.

Ryan stroked at a medium pace with Faith. Her body was so slim and perfect. It felt like she was gliding with him as he dove into her honey pot. After a few minutes of compassion, he started to increase his speed. Her nookie talked to him with every stroke.

Sliding out of her kitty, he gently kissed it and then flipped her over. Faith was healthy and proportionate with her ass. Her bright curves hypnotized his mind before he slid back in her water. When she adjusted to his aggression, she began to throw that ass in a circle. After all the late night sneaking and freaking, she became a pro. Arching Faith over more, Ryan dipped in her.

"Ahhh fuck, Ryan!"

"I love you," he grunted as she began to cream heavily.

"Damn. I love you too, nigga." She clawed at the sheets.

Gripping her waist, he unleashed his muscle and pumped in-side her roughly. A hand slammed across her ass cheek.

"Shittt," he mumbled as her coochie began to tighten around him. He busted a long nut into her backside. He could feel Faith release her orgasm with a light pant. He slow stroked to make sure he claimed his territory with that pussy.

Falling down next to him, she slapped his chest.

"You gon' stop just manhandling me, Ryan. My pussy hurts." She pouted her lips.

"My job is done then." He laughed.

* * *

Cheek Raw's spot, Newcastle

DJ, Wicked, and Reckless decided to get away for a little bit. The shit Ryan pulled was too hot and they didn't needed to be pointed out of a lineup for their recent lick. Deciding to sort the bricks out from Tech, they all gathered around to wait for Ryan, but unfortunately he was a no show. Still being loyal, they placed his cut to the side. It was wise to always do good business in order to see a good mission succeed.

Even this Cheek was a block nigga. He wasn't local like the people thought. He gave them the rundown on who their clientele would be. The crew listened with closed mouths.

"My plug is different. He's not the average guy. If we talking about being in this league, y'all better drop the young dumb shit right now. We can't come playing. These people will make your shit change in a blink. So it's up to y'all."

"If we eating, I wouldn't give a fuck. Make it happen," DJ agreed.

"Cool." Sitting back with a rolled blunt, DJ sparked it. He knew that Ryan was thrown off track by Raekwon's death, but the way he murked the old head in front of the entire neighbor-hood threw everyone for a loop. The entire section of Wilmington knew who splatted that boy, but the rats never made it in their neighborhood. It was now the topic of discussion. Females in school were gossiping around his name. Even the dopeboys were sending whispers around. They spoke about Ryan in the streets, and that shit wasn't good. Since his father was gone, words of Ryan taking the northside was being spread. In the projects, it wasn't about the money, only the body count. Ryan was the one stepping up to that plate.

* * *

DJ, a few weeks later

DJ drove down the street in his new black 96 Impala. The rain cascaded down DJ's windshield. He had already got off the three bricks he was given and ready to double up on a new pack. His shit moved so quick that he didn't have time to keep the paper in order. He still hadn't seen Ryan in weeks, and sitting home with Rose was getting boring. Even though the paper route was in motion, DJ and

Rose continued to attend school every day. It was the last year and they were determined to graduate .Of course, he kept his usual method of staying low key. He purchased Rose a few gifts to show his appreciation. Her love was well-needed when it came to surviving with the demons of Delaware.

DJ made his way from the east side towards the west. By the time he was across town, swerving down 8th and Adams, he spotted Ryan sitting in the breezeway with a hoodie over his head. He pulled in and Ryan hopped into the passenger seat.

"Wassup, D?" His voice sounded like he was depressed.

"Shit, man. I got that work for you, bro."

"Word. I didn't even want the work. That's why I threw it all on you."

"Nah, Ryan. You got a kid on the way, bruh. I'd rather see my niece or nephew eat before me." DJ threw the bag in to his lap. "Talk to me. What's been good for the past few days?

"Shit, bro. I just been laying low ever since that shit with Kil-la's stupid ass. I know I ain't get a chance to tell you, but I'm not trying to put none of us in a sticky mix. But if our respect dies, we die."

"I see, my nigga. Everybody been talking about that bullshit."

"Word?" Ryan asked.

"Yeah. Niggas saying you want yo' dad spot and all that oth-er shit."

"Well, they thought right. I ain't playing no more, DJ. In order to receive the shit we truly deserve, we have to break rules. Everyone has done it since the beginning of time. All they gotta do is fall in line and let us get our money."

"I know, bruh. But listen. We don't need no unwanted atten-tion. Niggas know what it is now. Let's get back to building a fortune," DJ told him sincerely.

"I know, bro. I know. I just lost it for a minute .I'm not on the hot shit. Only if it's necessary. You the only nigga that knows my situation." Ryan tapped his shoulder.

"Trust me, nigga, I know that feeling. I can't even look into my mom's eyes no more. The fact her and my dad strung out on crack makes it even worse. That shit makes me wanna kill every-thing in sight." DJ balled up his face angrily. "But guess what, bro? I got a team to think about now, so my feelings is out the window. That's because I'm Rich and Royal."

"I already know." Ryan nodded

"How Faith been?" DJ looked at a cop car that sat at the red light.

"She good. I just snatched her up a li'l whip so she can move around."

"Bet. This shit about to shoot through the roof. Trust me. You took me in like a brother when I didn't have noth-ing. We gon' take this shit over together. But we don't turn our backs on each other."

He gave him a pound.

Chris Green

Chapter 9

Wicked and Reckless's spot, Brookmont

For the past few days, Wicked had been laid under Tyleema. At first, it was to make their move for the control. The next lick was sweet, and Reckless wanted dibs on the paper before anyone could decide on splitting anything.

After spending some time with her, Wicked knew that she was a real one. She showed up every day after Reckless present-ed her the opportunity to make more money on the flip side. Her money hungry ways led her to agree, and shit was finally being perfected. Besides those fetish ways for plotting on some shit, she was a beautiful woman. Wicked had never felt the energy of a black girl so powerful. Her book sense was outstanding, and she caught on to anything slick. It was the complete opposite of him.

Looking up at Reckless as he walked through the door, Wick-ed wasted no time grabbing the blunt from his hand.

"What's up, fool? I been blowing yo' shit up. We been trying to fill you in on what's next."

"My shit dead. Plus I been dealing with this stupid bitch." He pointed at Diamond.

"Reckless, you ain't gotta talk to me like that. I'm not a hoe or a freak you be dealing with." Her neck was slanging from side to side.

Without hesitation, he leaned over and slapped the spit out of her mouth. "I'll fucking kill you. Don't disrespect me. This ain't D.C., hoe."

"Yo, Reck. Chill the fuck out!" Wicked snapped as he and Tyleema looked on.

As he continued to pound away at Diamond's head, he was snatched back and tackled to the floor when Wicked decided to step in. "I said chill, nigga .Are you fucking high?"

"Nigga, fuck that. She acting dumb. I don't tolerate disre-spect." He pushed his cousin off of him and stood up. "If you ain't rocking the way I am, step!" Reckless yelled.

Scrambling off the couch, Diamond rushed out of the front door.

"I don't give a damn about respect, bro. She's a female. My mama and auntie never allowed that shit back home and it ain't finna start now."

Wicked stood in Reckless's face with a stern expression.

Tyleema looked at them both.

"Listen, this ain't the way business works. Y'all called me over here to see how this shit can get split up better. Just like y'all here for each other, I'm here for my girls. Y'all say that Ryan and Cheek Raw got too much control over the pie. How are we gonna solve that? Because right now, we just dealing with messy shit." Tyleema crossed her legs.

"It's not that Ryan is getting too much of anything because it's always been even with him. We just want something separate for us to eat. Reckless feel like Ryan don't really want to let us all the way through with these moves. How can we eat like that?" Wicked flopped down on the couch.

"Nigga, he do block us out on everything. We standing around waiting for moves when we can be out here bumping our own door. This shit easy. I live this life for real. Just because we fuck with a nigga don't mean we gotta wait until he say eat." Reckless's hands moved back and forth.

"Okay. Has any one of you confronted him about this?" Ty-leema asked.

Both of them remained quiet. A weird vibe came to the room and she knew where the conversation was probably about to lead.

"Look. If y'all want some money, you gotta either let this man know what y'all feeling like or handle business on your own. Either way, it's not gonna work if nobody is on the same page."

"I know. We wanna get this money. Simple. If it's meant for us to bust another move with Ryan, so be it. But right now, tell me some good that can benefit us in this room?" Reckless asked.

"OK then. This mark's name is Johnny…"

* * *

Sekoya's Spot

Crawling out of the hot tub, Sekoya wrapped herself inside her warm nightgown. She picked the lotion up from the dresser. She sat on the bed and applied some to her legs. Her thighs were smooth and she didn't have a blemish on her skin.

The "Ride or Die" song from Ace Hood began to ring out from her cell phone. Without hesitation, she picked it u and answered.

"Hey bitch. Where are you?"

"Just now leaving Wicked and Reckless's house. These niggas a trip," Tyleema replied. "I called yo' phone like thirty times."

"I was handling some business," she lied.

Sekoya didn't want to tell her friend that she was slick choos-ing on Ryan. His angry demeanor was more than attractive, plus he handled that business well. It was an all-around turn on.

"Oh. Well anyway, I just called to let you know that I got something lined up for some extra money. Of course we splitting down so I need you to put Teona on point. Keep this on the low too. I just got a little more scheming to do," Tyleema warned her.

"Sure thing, baby mama." Sekoya smiled before hanging up.

Hearing the sound of money always excited her. She knew that if Tyleema brought anything to the table, it was more than official. Her ways were so strategic. The quietness could throw the most off, but she never spoke on anything that wasn't accu-rate.

Thinking about the money that was being put in place, she di-aled Ryan's number.

"What's good, li'l one?" he answered.

"Li'l one? Sekoyyaaaa, nigga. Not little one." She rolled her eyes at the phone.

"Girl, shut up. You know what I mean. What's up?" He chuckled.

"I got something for us. Tyleema said that she's gonna fill me in on all the details later."

"Cool, but is it some real money?" Ryan questioned. The es-timation from the last jack move wasn't good count. Is it worth it?"

"Let me handle that play, boy. I'ma give you the info when Ty hits me back. Besides, you know I do this shit," she stated arrogantly.

"Oh yeah?"

"Facts."

"Well shut up and handle it then." Ryan laughed before hanging up.

Cheesing from his smart-ass mouth, Sekoya placed on a pair of shorts and a T-shirt. Looking at herself in the mirror, she envisioned Ryan standing behind her. He was a hard piece that she needed for that thug lovin'. If his mouth matched his sex game, then he would have a serious problem on his hands.

* * *

Ryan's Spot, 8th and Adams

Ryan sat in the living room of his apartment with DJ, Faith, and Rose. Ryan stood up and grabbed the second bottle of Remy.

"Listen. We been sitting back kickin' it all day. Y'all girls need to get home. Faith, you know that we got a doctor's ap-pointment tomorrow. Get out of here and get some sleep."

"Why you always trying to get rid of me?" She smacked her lips.

"Well, take yo' ass in the room then. I don't give a damn whether you stay or not. It's time for bed. We got a doctor's appointment," he repeated a little louder.

Grabbing Rose's hand, Faith stomped off to the room.

"Faith is starting to get attached to you. She's pregnant, nig-ga. It's natural for babies to make a woman do that." DJ lit his blunt.

"I know. I just love fucking with her. I can run my own shit now. Slapping ass and bossing shit around makes me feel like I'm an elder." Ryan laughed.

Spitting out the smoke, DJ choked with a hand on his chest. "Nigga, you stupid."

"Nah for real though. Sekoya hit me up and said that we got another one. Them bitches ain't playing for that dough."

"What she talking about?"

"Apparently she ain't got all the info yet, but it gotta be soon. She sound excited, like it's a real check. I already said that I ain't with that small bread shit. It gotta be worth it."

Inhaling on the kush, DJ tapped Ryan's leg. "Bro, you ain't thought about just selling the dope and just cut the robbing shit out? I mean, we really don't need to do that shit anymore. It ain't like we striking for no lotto money. Plus the drugs will bring that back triple times."

"True. I thought about that. I guess the thrill been getting to me. Rich and Royal needs all the dough." Ryan raised his gun.

"The money will come, but we don't need cops. Robbing will bring they ass out of the cut. I pictured us living the life, bro. Just stacking paper and balling out of control. Even with Rose and Faith, they didn't want to be a part of this life. But it's still our job to take care of them."

"After this, we can drop the robbing for good. I was thinking hard also. I been doing my thing with this dope. I didn't really like hustling because I don't deal with this shit. I'm only smoking weed. I know you're more of the hustler, so our plans can go far if you're standing beside me. Cheek turning me on to a few cats soon. They gon' link up and shop with us. If they try to go around that, they die."

"Why?" DJ asked, confused.

"Because. I learned early in this game that if you ain't shop-ping with me, you plotting on getting me. It's a strategy. If we place the fear in these dumb-ass niggas, they gon' know not to cross us. It's a part of it. I'm only getting rid of motherfuckers who have the potential to be a problem," Ryan stated before sipping his bottle.

"I agree. Just be cautious. I don't wanna be sitting in no cell for the rest of our lives, dawg. We got the way and shit is about to get beyond great. We ain't letting nobody underhand us. I ain't disguising myself as no fucking killer. I've done it, and I'll do it again if I have to. We all that matter." DJ rolled up another joint.

Soaking his boy's words in, Ryan closed his eyes. He envi-sioned them living it up. The thought of his seed being born to a rich father was all he prepared himself for. After all, you couldn't be Rich without being Royal.

* * *

Two days later

Sitting outside of the lick's house, Reckless and Wicked waited for their sign to push up inside that bitch. They never knew that Ryan and DJ were already stationed on the side of his home. The night sky was hawking fast, and soon it would be easy for Johnny to spot the cars that had already been sitting outside of his crib for the past two hours.

Wicked waited patiently with his guns in hand. All he could think about was Tyleema. The thought of her bouncing on anoth-er nigga's dick made him catch a slight attitude. The past week was so great with her that he felt no one could have possession over her anymore. Still and all, Tyleema told him that when it came to getting money, she would do whatever it took.

Hearing the text slide in to his phone, he looked down at the message. It was her, and they just gave the green light to push in.

"Let's go!" Wicked jumped out of the car with Reckless directly behind him.

Running through the yard, they headed for the back door. After reaching the next corner of Johnny's home, Wicked and Reckless ran directly into Ryan and DJ.

"What the fuck? Where did y'all niggas come from?" Reck-less stopped in his tracks with a confused face.

"What the fuck are you talking about? Keep going," DJ whis-pered while pushing him towards the back door.

Trailing behind each other like a military crew, they stormed through the back door, following Ryan's direction.

* * *

Sekoya sucked on Johnny's rod while he stood in front of her. Getting on her knees beside her, Teona kissed Sekoya before tasting his manhood. The feel of the two gorgeous women aroused him.

Tyleema sat on the couch with his homeboy. His fingers were inside her jeans and their tongues connected every time he pushed them inside of her.

The mood was lit and the liquor had the room tipsy. Sekoya's eyes landed on Ryan creeping through the hallway in front of them.

"Get the fuck on the ground!" Reckless yelled.

The sound of his voice caused everybody to panic. The girls did their job and dropped straight to the floor.

Johnny was struggling with his pants and fell down to the floor. "Nigga, stop pointing the gun at me. You might shoot me, fool. Just tell me who did it and I'll handle it," he screamed out of fear with his arms wrapped around his head.

"Please don't hurt us!" Sekoya shouted with a fake per-for-mance.

"Shut up, bitch!" Reckless barked.

Wicked wasting no time sliding his pistol on Tyleema's vic-tim. "That goes for you too, pussy."

"Everybody calm the fuck down," Ryan ordered.

Bending down in front of John, he tapped his leg with the gun. "Aye buddy, I need you to look at me so we can be clear on this."

"Are you gonna shoot me, man?" His hands slowly came down to his side.

"I don't know. Do you got something I might need in this crib? Because if not, I'm gonna shoot you," Ryan said seriously.

"What the fuck, big dog? I don't even know you, man. I'm just a li'l playa from the east, man." His hands trembled and he observed everyone who was in the room.

"Answer my question. This shit can go the same way the movies end. I'ma lose my patience, shoot you in the head, kill all these hoes, and tear this bitch up to get what I need."

Taking a deep breath, Johnny panted. The barrel of Ryan's gun dangled at the tip of his skull. When he clicked the hammer back, Johnny screamed. "The kitchen, man! It's in the trash can!"

"Damn, you know how to count. I was just about to pull this bitch. Reckless, get the paper."

Doing what he was told, Reckless backtracked to re-trieve the money.

"Y'all bitches get the fuck up. Put on yo' clothes and get the fuck out. Now!" Ryan ordered.

Tyleema, Sekoya, and Teona jumped to their feet quickly, shuffling to get their things. They rushed out of the house, leav-ing Johnny for dead.

"I know this may be an inconvenience for you, but I need it."

Just as Ryan made the statement, Reckless stepped back into the room. "I got it. This bitch filled to the top."

A black Adidas bag was strapped around his back. Turning back to Johnny, Ryan laughed. "Thanks for your time. I'm gonna leave you with your spirit. That should make us even. Let's go, y'all." He turned around to leave.

Wicked was the only one who stood in place. Ever since he spotted Johnny's homeboy next to Tyleema, he waited for his opportunity. His gun was still pointed and the man looked on with an angry expression. It was a look of revenge. His eyes studied Wicked, and that's when it happened.

"Wicked. Let's go." Ryan stopped to see what the fuck was on his mind.

Before he could repeat it, Wicked snapped, tapping his trigger twice. The slugs found their home in his throat, sending him to the floor. Turning around with their guns in the air, the crew ran to his side.

"What the fuck is wrong with you, nigga? Why you do that?" DJ pushed him.

"Fuck that shit, nigga. I'm a grown-ass man. He bucked back."

"I'm sick of this shit. Y'all niggas busting for the hell of it. Scary-ass nigga. If you want to catch a body, you do it by your-self." DJ was clutching his gun while standing in Wicked's face.

"Get the fuck out of my cousin's face, nigga!" Reckless stepped forward.

"What the fuck y'all niggas got on y'all mind?" Ryan jumped in the middle. "Snap back to reality, and I mean quick." He looked around at all of them.

They were in the middle of a robbery, and things had taken a wrong turn.

"Fuck that shit. I'm done. Since y'all niggas wanna shoot shit for fun, I'm finished after this lick. From now on, y'all can rock alone with it," DJ said.

DJ turned around to look at Johnny squirming on the floor and placed three shots into his body before walking out.

Shaking his head, Ryan followed with Wicked and Reckless in front of him. The mission was a success with a slight failure. Arguing about paper was something that wasn't allowed. The stunt that Reckless tried to pull wasn't sitting right with Ryan. There was surely a problem cooking in the air.

* * *

Pulling back up to his apartment, Ryan and DJ climbed out of the car with Reckless and Wicked directly behind them. The girls sat around the living room sharing a drink. After the move, they were able to jump back in their whip to make it back across town. It was supposed to be a smooth caper.

"What the fuck just happened back there?" Ryan set his gun on the table.

The girls sat up from the couch to see what the he'll was going on.

"Nigga, I blowed that nigga shit off because I wanted to. Don't tell me how to rock. That's all I'm saying." Wicked looked over to DJ.

"That's understandable. But you had no purpose."

"You didn't have a purpose when you blamed Killa in the middle of the day either, Ryan. I didn't question you. I just accepted it and kept it moving," he reminded him.

Reckless stood over in the corner with an aggravated look on his face. The money was still around his back.

"I'm saying, nigga. You got something on yo' mind?" Ryan checked him.

"Hell yeah, I do."

"Well, speak then. You a man, right?"

"This was my move nigga. Where the hell did y'all even come from?"

"Your move? What the fuck made you feel like this was your mission alone, nigga? We a team." DJ rose to his feet.

"Like I said, I worked this out for me and Wicked to get some extra money. When we came around the house, I didn't expect to see y'all. This was only for us." He exposed the entire ordeal.

"Wait a minute. First off, I don't give a damn what you thought. This shit ain't just for you. Wherever you heard that shit, they lied to you. If y'all niggas don't wanna get paper with us, fine. We ain't stopping ya. But that paper getting split up be-tween all seven of us. Right now." He held his hand out for the bag around Reckless's neck.

His heart wanted to buck against the slick talk so bad. Wick-ed looked over to him, knowing where his cousin's mind was. The entire stunt was pulled totally wrong and now it was being thrown out in the air for a conclusion. There was no more time to think. If Reckless started a gun fight in the midst of Ryan's spot because of the paper, it would leave Wicked without a choice but to ride with his flesh and blood.

Instead of bucking against the ruling, Reckless took the bag from around his neck and tossed it over to Ryan, giving him a stern nod. He poured the cash out on the coffee table.

An hour that passed before he finished adding up the loot, sliding everybody their cut. The girls split, leaving the four of them in the house alone.

"So let's put this out on the table. Me and DJ ain't laying nig-gas down no more. Tonight was it. Since y'all wanna make decisions on your own, we ain't doing no more jacking. We selling this work. Either you down or not. If you ain't, get the hell on and do you." Ryan confronted every last one of them.

"First off, I love y'all niggas, bro. But bro is my family. We can all eat and be a better team together. Everybody not meant to be no dope boy, Ryan." Wicked stepped up to say something first.

"Well, robbing ain't about to be the Rich and Royal motto. We sell weight now. This is where you see that ain't no option. We can fuck with each other, but I'm done with that shit until it's a real meal where everybody can eat."

"Well, I'm out. I'm robbing until I can't no more. I want my shit easy, and that's what I know. I grew up laying niggas down from Arizona to Delaware. That's me and what I'm standing on," Reckless said before taking his cut of the money. He left the apartment, slamming the door behind him.

"Fuck you gon' do?" Ryan asked Wicked with a crooked mug.

He couldn't believe that shit had flopped over so fast. The money was the reason everybody was disconnected in Wicked's eyes.

"Ryan, we ride together, bro. Just know that it ain't no sepa-ration in my heart. I'm still the same, period. We just gonna let shit blow over until we can put this shit back to-gether."

Wicked embraced both of them with a handshake. He left behind Reckless.

DJ looked at Ryan when the door closed behind him. "Didn't I tell you them niggas on some slime shit? They ain't been acting right since them bitches came in the picture. Wicked is bugging off that little hoe Tyleema."

"Them niggas wanna control some shit, bro. If you ain't meant to lead, step to the side. I ain't letting nobody crash this shit. If they wanna act like it's a competition, I'll smoke they ass just like the rest. I hate to feel that way, but before they cross us, they'll die. If robbing is what them niggas feel like doing, fine. If business between us go sour for any reason after this, I'm murk-ing shit and asking questions after." Ryan was pouring up a cup of Hennessy.

"I seen this shit from a mile away. Them boys feeling they self. Reckless has tried to pump himself up to be like you. Be-sides following behind him, ain't shit wrong with Wicked. He don't even wanna be on the opposite side of us."

"That's the beauty of it, DJ. Nothing can stop the truth. When you have fuck-ass motives, your cards will still fall horribly. It's the same reason I'm uncut and tell mu'fuckas what it is. I'm not hiding it. That's what makes me a real G. I seen just in these few days of hustling that I can run up a real bank account. I want this city, DJ. But quietly." Ryan sat back at the table.

"We can do it. The product isn't the problem. We ain't toting no two hundred bricks. We still on three. All we gotta do is stay out the way and suck up the bread. Fuck all the rest of that other shit, Ryan. I'm tired of backtracking for small stuff when we already know how this shit works.

I got all the good shit in my mind and if we pump this shit back up, I'm going to lose it. I been through a lot too, bro. That shit humbled me so I know that we can do the meter on this game. We don't need to be slacking for nothing. You know I'm standing right here, even if we be the two last shooters. When this real plug drop in, the turf gone respect us." DJ rose to his feet.

"Guess what? It's known. And all I cared about was the squad from the jump. Niggas will play they self out of pocket. I'ma just put them back in that bitch."

After they embraced each other with a brotherly hug, DJ tossed on his coat. "I'ma hit you tomorrow, bro. I know Rose is probably about to commit suicide." He smiled before leaving.

"Later." Ryan replied.

He jumped up from the table, locked his door, and retired back to the couch. Looking around the spacious apartment, he nodded at the smooth set up. Flat screens and suede couches were the usual, but this spot had a different vibe. It was more refreshing than anything. After the ten months was up, Cheek Raw could have his spot back because Ryan was moving for the big league.

* * *

Cheek Raw, 1:40 p.m., October 2nd

Cheek was posted down on 5th and Monroe with his young homies, shooting a round of dice. After swiping up a few more dollars, he sat back and waited for the traffic to die down. The expressway was packed during the afternoon and he needed to cross town before it got late. His

Givenchy shirt was crispy. The white jeans he wore were knitted by Alexander McQueen and his shoes were a pair of original number 11 Jordan's. The recent check from Ryan and his team paid off nicely. The block was sliding cakes out of the trap by the load and things were better than ever with his new connections.

Cheek was so busy running his mouth to some sluts that he didn't peep the dark blue Lexus across the street watching his movements.

"Yeah, I been doing this shit. Y'all just learning." He spread his money to flex for the small circle that stood around talking with him.

All eyes were on Cheek as the people moved around the thugged out block.

"That's him, ain't it?" Baltimore clutched his gun.

"Yeah. That's him. His bitch ass thinks he's the shit." Severe mugged him with his twin Glocks tucked.

Cheek was moving in the parking lot of the spot with free will. He didn't know that they were ready to bust his entire brain when the opportunity presented itself.

"How you want me to do it? I'll just shoot all of them." He looked over in Severe's eyes.

"Wait a second."

Sitting back, he observed the niggas that were standing with him. Pistols hung on all their waists. Their faces weren't moving, neither were they enjoying themselves. The one thing he knew about Cheek was his street tactics. He was known to keep some niggas on go every second of the day. At least one was always lurking around just to ensure that he wouldn't have to watch his back. He was a known loud head that wanted to be heard. He would shine on everybody just to show what he could do. It was always his image. Ever since he called his little goons to run the streets, they slashed his paper out of the picture and caused problems that they weren't prepared to face. Johnny was mur-dered and Supreme was putting the press on Cheek's head being rocked from his shoulders. He felt that Cheek was just a snotty nose shooter who didn't have any manners. It was a selfish act of how he disrespected the one's over him. But it was still suicide to send his young hitta out there when the sharks were swimming deep. He would only have so long before his time clicked to an end.

Severe was a hilltop nigga from 6th and Franklin. He was no longer seeing any money, thanks to Cheek Raw. All the fiends that used to cop from him where now receiving shit straight from his block. The mutual respect was even, but the line was crossed when he had spilled Johnny's blood. The talk about his pure cocaine quality was obviously true. The people moved about like they were stopping for a quick cup of Starbucks's finest mocha.

"When you trying to handle this nigga?" Baltimore asked with an urge to pull a trigger.

"You move too fast, li'l nigga. Patience. All you have to do is wait for the perfect time. It always comes," Severe responded before pulling away from the block.

Chapter 10

DJ's new spot, Newcastle

After pleasing Rose for a few hours, DJ jumped out of the shower and decided to catch a movie with his queen. She was being overbearing ever since he came home, but it only showed him that she was indeed in need of some hard attention. He had no choice but to beat the pussy to submission.

After cuddling for a few minutes, Rose rubbed his cheek. "Baby, have you ever thought about having kids?"

He looked at her with a raised eyebrow. He turned his head back to the flat screen. "Nah, not yet."

"Really, DJ, you ain't never thought about our family? I need at least three children. I thought you was ready to marry me. We can't have a relationship without kids," she complained.

"Rose, you've been around Faith a little too much. Just be-cause you see her all happy and shit about this baby don't mean that it's all good. When it comes down to taking care of that seed, you can't pick when to spend that bread on them. We so self-centered with small feelings that a baby could even make us fall apart. We have to make sure we're set in order to bring another life into this world." DJ reached over to the night stand for his weed.

"I'm not worried about Faith's baby. Her and Ryan doing what they do. I was just speaking on what I wanted for the near future. I'm not trying to be the bride of a hustla like a Destiny Skai novel nigga. These streets ain't giving no foundation to build what we need either. I don't care how much money we have."

"You right, but now we just in grind mode. Lately I been thinking about a lot of shit we want, and don't make it seem like I'm not interested in what you want, because I am. I just know what it takes to win. This shit about to be bigger than you think. I gotta be able to make sure I can give you the world before I can raise my kid. How many daddies you know at school taking care of those real deal father duties? Those girls were mothers before they could grow from being a child themselves. When we have our family, it'll be the one you've always dreamed of," DJ explained humbly enough to not hurt her feelings.

Rolling over on her stomach, Rose stared at him. "So what about choosing your friends wisely? I don't want to see you be the next Ryan or Raekwon. Delaware ain't big enough for every killer and you know that. It's niggas on the east side murdering people by the day. That's not my mission on identifying your body because of a reputation. That leaves me with no family or no husband," Rose spoke genuinely.

DJ knew that shit was the absolute truth. Sitting in the shad-ows waiting for a spot could lead to you being taken out in the process. Nothing was gonna make him choose that chance over the fam.

"Rose, I know shit be hard sometimes. We come from a mind frame that every white man is the bad guy. No one sends their kids in the world and lets them know that it's no such thing as love. They feel that someone giving them something is the key to winning. No one means more than you. I can't fuck the streets out of nothing but paper. No panties. And I'm damn sho' not gay. So a nigga is the last thing you're gonna lose me to. I move this way for one reason, Rose: to make sure that shit in place for the next day. Trust me, I got you." he said before kissing her soft lips.

* * *

Precious

Ryan strolled through the mall, purchasing a few new things before he completed his wardrobe. After all his priorities were in order, he took care of himself with a small spree on fashion. Clothes and shoes was his way of dressing to impress. Different shit for different moods. You wasn't nothing if you didn't match the image of yo' talk game. The people wouldn't match with you. Respect was only for the ones who could spread the love and take care of themselves in the process.

Standing at the counter inside of the Fendi clothing store, Ryan felt a light tap on his shoulder. Turning around, his eyes landed on the girl he had met in the shoe store a few months prior. Her beautiful hair was neatly straightened down past her shoulders. Her dark brown eyes studied him with joy and slight nervousness, and her dimples dug deeper every time Ryan blinked his eyes to look her up and down

"What's good, ma? Long time no see."

"I was about to say the same thing to you. You never got a chance to even learn anything about the college courses I take."

He remembered the number she wrote on his shoe receipt. So much was going on that she slipped totally out of his mind. "Yeahhh, I was gonna get around to calling you, but I misplaced your number. How has the school thing been going for you anyway?" He looked at the sweatpants hugging her body. The small college T-shirt gave her the innocent schoolgirl look. Her smile was just so amazing.

"Well, I'm finally done with school. I graduated two weeks ago and I've opened my own business. I'm an investor. I've signed up for another three years for a higher business and mar-keting degree so my pay grade will rise with every semester. You need to think of stuff you want to do for yourself, business wise. It's good to have your own in the case of building an empire for your kids or loved ones."

Hearing the word "kid" caused Faith to pop in his mind. A baby would surely need an empire if you didn't want to suffer with a struggle. It was never a guarantee when working for another. But a legit business was the key, something that Ryan didn't have knowledge of. "What type of businesses?"

"I mean like real estate, franchises, restaurants, even these same clothing stores you buy from like this one," Precious schooled him.

"You sound like you got this down pat. Let's say if I had some money to invest. How would that work?" Ryan stared into her eyes.

She could feel a sense of domination in his face. He was hungry for something, and she wanted to help him achieve it, if that was his true intention. "You mean like a partnership?" She smiled.

He couldn't help but blush at her forwardness. "Yes, if that's what you want. What will it take?"

"Well, that depends on what we want to do. We could start small and work our way up after we form a plan to see what we're investing in. Did you have anything in mind?"

Thinking to himself, he folded his arms. "Houses."

"Okay. We can start off with looking up foreclosed homes. I'll get the information and we can have a sit-down to see where to head. I'll do some research for you tonight if you like." Pre-cious was twirling on her foot.

Ryan pulled a wad of cash out his pockets. He counted out a quick five thousand. "We should be able to start a bank account with this. Whenever we sit down to think of what you wanna do, I'll put the money up for it." Ryan placed the money in her palms.

Staring down at the cash, she smirked. "How you gon' give me the money and still ain't called so we can put this together? You already decreased our profits in this little time."

"We partners now though. I don't let my business partners down, period."

Reaching into his pocket, she removed his phone and saved her number in the contacts. Placing it up to his face, she showed him her name. "You can't lose this phone like that paper. Hope-fully you can use it this time."

"I will. We got business, remember?" Ryan flirted with his eyes.

As he watched her stroll out of the store, he scanned her body up and down. If she continued to smell so good and look so damn good, she would be more than just a business partner. Friendships were great to build because there was never no telling when you would need to spread your wings and switch it up.

That was the thing about being the man. You had options.

* * *

When he got back to his crib, Ryan tossed his new clothes on the side of his bed. So much bread was laying around the streets and he couldn't wait to swipe it up. He pulled a duffle from his closet. He set on the bed and poured out his stash. After counting up the stacks, he added up a cool hundred and fifty bands. It wasn't quick, but after finding a balance on saving, he began to rise swiftly. He glared at all the money. He thought about Kimyetta. Day after day, he would call her line to see if he could just hear her voice once. After the news with his father hit, she had packed her things and left. He hated the fact that she wouldn't let him live, but in the end, Ryan didn't want to sever the kinship with the woman who birthed him.

Dialing her number on his phone, he listened as it rang in his ear. Feeling that he was about to get the same results, he nearly pressed the end button.

"Hello?" she picked up.

"Mama?"

"Hey Ryan. How are you?" Kim asked sincerely.

"I'm okay. Why haven't you picked up the phone for me in months? You know that I've been worried about you," he ques-tioned.

"Because I'm scared for you, boy. Don't you get it, Ryan? You're making a bed that I don't want to see you lay in. I'm your mom, not your girlfriend. I can't tell you what you wanna hear. Your dad's death woke me up, Ry. How we gon' love each other if we all dying?" Kimyetta asked.

Respecting her words, he huffed into the phone, "I know, Ma. All I wanted to do was make sure we were good. Nobody loves you more than me. You know that. I can't help what I'm good at, Ma."

"Yeah, but you can help it if it's something that's killing you, baby. Ryan, everyone who me and your dad grew up with is dead. The crew he ran with is dead. It's only two ways to go out, and you've been preached that since the beginning of time. Come move out here with me, Ryan. I can't watch you do what your father did."

After sitting in silence, he finally answered. "I can't right now, Mama .I'm really trying to do something that will benefit both of us forever. You have to trust me," he begged her.

"Well, do it by yourself, bitch. When you ready to come home to me without all that street shit, I'll be waiting. Besides that, I don't have anything to say, Ryan." She hung up in his ear.

It was clear that their conversation had been heading for that. Unfortunately, emotions were something that couldn't affect his decision. All his sacrifices had led to that exact moment, and it was surely for a purpose.

Calling a different number, he placed the phone to his ear. After a few rings, it was answered.

"Hellooo?"

"Now teach me all this business stuff that I'm supposed to know." Ryan sat back on the bed with a pen and paper in hand.

Giggling, Precious shuffled on the other side of the phone. "Where do you wanna start?"

"With loyalty," he replied before smirking.

Chapter 11

Cheek Raw, down bottom, W.5th Street, the next day

Standing down on the block, Cheek moved about with a few members of his team. Today was past special. It was more epic than anything. He finally got his chance to run in the big league, and meeting the man was at the top of his list. Ever since he linked in with Ryan, the extra weight and money from the rob-beries were setting him straight.

Looking out into the street, he spotted the all-black tinted Durango. It was third time it passed within the last thirty minutes. It was natural in the hood to raise suspicion on a vehicle that was never seen. His crew was already on point. But making the block hot would have to be for a reason. If a nigga wanted smoke, he would get it. But they still had to be prepared if it was the biggest enemy: the police.

He watched the car slide over towards the sidewalk. It stopped, and the front window rolled down.

"Yo Cheek. What's good with it, bro?" the driver said.

"What's up, old head? Why the hell you surfing around? You could have been pulled up," he responded, stepping closer.

"Because I wanted you to remember me."

The remark froze Cheek's feet as the back window slightly lowered. The barrel of an AR-15 assault rifle slid through and began to blow like a trumpet.

Pak! Pak! Pak! Pak! Pak!

Cheek fell to the ground and bounced up faster than a cat, pulling his strap. He shot recklessly behind him. His feet were moving so fast that he nearly tripped twice. The three men who stood with him tried to retaliate, but suffered a horrible fate. The cop killer bullets inside of the machine Swiss cheesed their bodies before a gun could be removed. Instead of the little homie Sheen busting back, he caught flight faster than a missile at war. He didn't even care about his friends being slaughtered because he wasn't making a dime off of anything they were doing.

After leaving the block full of smoke and shells, the Durango smashed off through the streets of Delaware.

Still running down the back street of 5th, Cheek entered the parking lot of the corner store and ran inside. He headed for the back where the gambling machines rested. Catching his breath, he took a seat and watched the police cruisers fly down to the block.

The thought of a nigga trying to ambush him placed fire in his soul. There was nobody on the north with enough courage to try Cheek in such a disrespectful manner. His associates alone proved that he could get a nigga touched for playing stupid.

Cheek pulled out his cell. He wiped the sweat from his brow and dialed Ryan's number. His eyes continued to watch more cop cars float down 5th.

"What's good, Cheek?"

"Ryan, I need you to come get me. I'm down at the corner store on the bottom. A nigga just shot at me." He fumed with anger while checking his body for gun wounds.

"What?

"Yeah, young bull. Pull up. How far are you from here? It's too many police flying around and I need to move before they start locking shit down."

"I'm like five minutes away from there. I'm coming now."

Cheek hung up, checked the bullets in his clip, and placed it back on his hip. After purchasing a pack of Newport's, he lit one and stared out at the street. Citizens headed for 5th as if a celeb-rity bash was on set in the hood. Cheek saw Ryan's Q35 Infiniti truck. He made his way quickly out of the store's entrance and jumped into the passenger seat.

"What the fuck happened?" Ryan asked, pulling out of the lot. "It's cars crawling all down in the bottom. They got caution tape around that motherfucker."

"A nigga tried they luck and missed. I'm placing tags on brains for the high price."

"Do you know who did it?

"An old head I used to serve pulled up. But it wasn't nobody in the passenger seat. He said some weird shit to me like, 'I'ma make sure you remember me.' It was creepy as fuck. Before I could peep it, the back window let down and somebody started squeezing on us. They killed Boogie and Jbo. Sheen caught flight," Cheek said while leaning his head back on the seat. "You can just drop me off in Newark."

"Cool," Ryan replied while shaking his head.

Heading to the opposite end of the crime scene, they jumped on the expressway.

"So what you gon' do about it?" Ryan asked curiously.

"Handle that business and show niggas why my name Cheek Raw."

* * *

Sekoya's spot

Walking through the door of her home, Sekoya looked at Ty-leema and Teona, who sat on the couch with a bottle of Moet. The air smelled like they were burning weed with a mixture of something that didn't mix.

Sniffing the aroma in the air, she walked over to both of them.

"Teona! What the fuck did I say about smoking that shit in my house?"

"Girl, relax. That shit been gone. If I put cocaine in my weed, that's my business. Not yours," she snapped back.

"You heard what I said, bitch." Turning her attention to Ty-leema, she folded her arms. "Why didn't you tell me that Johnny worked for Supreme?"

"Because it didn't matter. It's not like we robbed him, Sekoya."

"Bitch, he works for Supreme. Anything that nigga had in his crib probably wasn't even his shit. Why would you do that when you know I don't cross that type of line with him, Tyleema?"

"Supreme ain't studding you, girl. Y'all ain't even together no more. How you gon' let that nigga control the way you eat?" She was getting aggravated.

"It's not about that. He's dangerous, Ty. If that man finds out that we had anything to do with that shit, we could be ended. Did you know Cheek Raw got shot at today?

"And?

"And? He knows I deal with Cheek on licks. I'm not trying to be out here beefing with Supreme about shit. We could get hurt, Tyleema."

"All you have to do is relax. We gonna be good. We got enough money to eat off right now, plus we got Cheek's team moving with us. They got our back." She stumbled to her feet.

"We ain't living a movie script, bitch. Supreme has money to touch yo' ass way in Australia. These are some fucking high school kids!" Sekoya shouted.

"Really? So why you trying yo' best to please this nigga Ryan? Put his ass on game. If that nigga tries us, we can lick his ass and let them pull what they been doing. Them little niggas ain't sparing shit when we go in them cribs, and his ass can get it the same way."

Shaking her head, Sekoya strolled to her bedroom. Supreme was an older cat who was the boss of bosses. He didn't mind sharing the wealth, but he didn't play about making it. At that time, he was the king in Delaware. Nothing could be purchased through the city border line unless he received a cut.

Sekoya wasn't fearful of Supreme, but she was just his wife-to-be. He treated her like shit for years until she finally had enough courage to bounce. Regardless of the things he could offer, she couldn't put up with the abuse. After striking for half of his safe, she left his home and hid throughout the streets until he tracked her down. After beating her in front of the entire block, he decided to let her stay exactly where she wanted to be: in the streets. The only thing she worried about was the news he would receive on the vicious act. If the girls' names were any-where involved, she knew that a closed door to her past would surely be reopened.

* * *

Severe, Hampton Hotel

"That nigga dead," Severe said through the line as he looked out of the large hotel window.

"Yeah, that's excellent news. Now the real feast can begin," Supreme replied.

"Listen, I know this shit been rocky out here lately and the trust market is out of business, big dawg, but I'm ready. I feel like we can run these blocks 24/7."

"That ain't important right now to me. The block has been mines, Severe. The mission for my organization is to crush all competition out of the way. You understand how the Delaware tradition goes. We don't fight for blocks. We fight for hoods. If niggas make it hard, I flip it and make it easy. How many of them left?"

"It's like four of them. They some young bulls though. I think it's Ryan and DJ. Them the names they stressing in the streets .I never knew that was Raekwon's son."

"Raekwon?"

"Yeah, he has a son named Ryan. That's the one who taking his gun game to the extreme on the north."

"Fuck Raekwon! I know he's long gone, and his son is gonna be next. Take care of them people quietly. I don't need interrup-tions in my business, Severe. It causes me to get angry. Find out the names of all they little friends and handle them accordingly," Supreme ordered.

"Don't worry. I'm the man for the mission." Severe hung up with a smile.

"What did he say?" Baltimore asked.

"He said that we were gonna be the new kings of fuck-ing Delaware. All we gotta do is have some patience and put in that work. You sure you seen that nigga die, cor-rect?"

"I watched him. A couple of his partnas ran for dear life, but I spanked three of them off top," he assured him.

"Great, 'cause with him gone, we hit the top," Severe said be-fore placing a call.

* * *

Cheek Raw, 9:00 p.m., Westside Elsemere Road

Cheek, Wicked, Reckless, and Ryan sat inside of the cargo van with their weapons loaded to the max. The disrespect that occurred with Cheek Raw had Ryan furious. It even brought Wicked and Reckless out on the bullshit. Cheek was more like an older brother to them all. The loss of his immediate squad was hard to swallow, and that was the reason Cheek called up his young bulls to get some answers.

Clutching onto the guns, they watched as Sekoya and Tyleema sashayed pass the three corner hustlers on the block, knowing how it would work if these niggas saw a fat loose ass. He had called the girls for a good decoy. Sekoya wasted no time agree-ing, especially when there were some bands involved.

"Here they go," Cheek alerted his young hittas.

Just as he suspected, those niggas followed right behind the girls. One continued to grab Tyleema's hand while the other walked beside Sekoya like he was too smooth and cool to walk on the ground. As they crossed in front of the van, the side door slid open and the crew jumped out, guns in the air.

"Put ya hands up, baby boy. Make sure you make it home to eat Mama's dinner," Cheek threatened with his gun on one of the men.

Ryan wasted no time throwing the first lame into the trunk. After Sekoya and Tyleema witnessed that, they both took off running back towards their car.

"Get in, nigga." Cheek Raw pushed the other victim inside before Wicked closed the sliding door behind him.

He walked back around to the driver's seat, hopped in, and pulled away from the street. His intentions were to kill them both on the block in front of whoever, but knowing how a kidnapping in Delaware could go, he switched up his action.

"Pull right there in that cut," Ryan pointed from the passenger side.

Swerving over, Cheek pulled the van inside of the stinky al-leyway on Maryland Avenue. The spot used to be a warehouse, but was shut down after the property was condemned.

They stepped out, pulled the men out, and pushed them into the dirty water on the concrete. Moving to the edge of the cut, Wicked stood to make sure that nobody entered until they were done.

"Now I had to come all this way for some shit that ain't even making no sense to me. Your name is Jye, right?" Cheek pointed the weapon at his head.

"Yeah, you know that. What's the meaning of this shit, Cheek? We on the same team," he stressed.

"Uh, obviously we not. Word on the street is y'all pussy-ass boss man shot at me. I need the address to him. Now."

"We ain't telling you shit!" the other man spat with anger. "Y'all niggas some rookies. We ain't coming off no money or - "

His talking ended with one squeeze of Ryan's SIG Sauer handgun.

Boom!

The blood that splattered from his homeboy's brain landed directly into his mouth. Cringing up his face from the sight, he closed his eyes and slightly shivered.

"He wasn't gon' be able to help. I already seen it," Ryan shrugged with a smile.

Snapping his head back to Jye, he pushed his strap into his lips. "Supreme. Where that nigga stay at?"

"That's fucked up how you rocking, Cheeks. I gotta be a snitch now?"

"If you wanna live. You'll oblige or end up like ya dog right here," he replied.

"12 Antioch Court, down in Newcastle."

"Newcastle? Why you just didn't say that the first time?"

Whipping out his small switchblade, Cheek jammed it into Jye's jaw repeatedly.

"Ahhh. Ahhh! Wait!"

Cheek continued to handle his business until Jye's entire cheek was detached. "Y'all pussies made the worst mistake gunning at me. Now y'all gon' see why they want me off the streets." He stood over the man as he shook uncontrollably.

"We out," Reckless said before leaving out of the cut.

Following behind one another, the guys climbed back into the van and left, heading back to the north.

Chris Green

Chapter 12

Detective Christopher Bradley, the shooting scene, 5th and Mon-roe

Stepping out of his unmarked truck, Detective Bradley crossed under the yellow tape. The scene was horrible. He had just arrived, and what he heard so far was about to start a major controversy. Asking around the block was pointless. For years, no one would speak about anything that happened in their sight. The citizens were scared straight. It was surely the same punks that terrorized the streets years before. It was the same cycle. The only thing that changed was the people.

Strolling over to where the bodies lay, he spotted the lieuten-ant. Showing his badge to the surrounding officers, he stepped over to him.

"Tell me what the hell is going on here?"

"Well, it seems like we had a gun fight. Apparently some bad guys rolled into the neighborhood, jumped out of the vehicle, shot the three victims. The weapon was an assault rifle. AR-15, maybe an AK-47 .Of course all of the neighbors claimed that they were asleep. A few people who were driving by claimed to see a few men flee the scene. That's about it," he replied.

"So you mean to tell me that three people were killed in broad daylight and nobody saw anything?

"Besides the few people in the store, nothing that's valuable. Still, they didn't want to give their names. Your partner Cross is in the store questioning the owner now."

Making his way across the street, he entered the store and headed over to his partner.

"Cross, is this helping you in any kind of way?"

"A little. The store manager said that they were shooting at a guy named Cheek or something like that. He doesn't know any of the other men."

Simmering on his name, Bradley cursed himself for ever let-ting him slide through the cracks. He was now becoming a major problem. "Ask him if they have a videotape."

"Already on it. He's pulling it for us now."

Every time that a problem occurred in the area, Cheek Raw's name was ringing a hundred bells. The radar for him was beyond red. After tearing down the city with his pollution and violent influence, he became voted most likely for a prison cell and a life sentence.

"Bradley, do you think this is some type of retaliation about that Johnny kid? It seems like a lot of smoke has been in the air since. The chief is saying we might have a war on our hands."

"There ain't no damn war. If it was, these fools would be running around like it was the day of resurrection. This is some-thing personal, especially if it has anything to do with Raw. I need you to tell forensics to run prints on every shell they found. I need a twenty-four hour squad for these crews hanging on the sidewalks. Lock all their asses up, at least long enough to where we can pull something out of them. I don't like showing back up at the office without good news. I got a solid identification of Raw at that scene as well. So the war is not smoking a damn thing if this son of bitch Cheek Raw ain't here. He can hide, but I'm the monster in the closet. He's gonna need more than a fucking scary killer of Delaware to stop me from hunting his ass down."

As they walked out of the store, a crime scene investigator stepped over to them. "Detective Bradley, we have discovered a weapon behind William Hicks Anderson community center. It could've possibly been used in this shooting."

"What makes you say that?

"Because there was only half a clip. We dusted it for prints to see if ballistics could match us to a body."

"Good." Bradley buttoned up his pea coat. "Maybe we can find one of these assholes. Clear out the apartments. I don't need anyone hanging around unless they're speaking about this triple homicide."

"Right away, sir." He walked back to his station across the street.

"Cross, I need you to operate the area tonight. I'll be in contact," Bradley said as he made his way back to the car.

After getting in his car, he sparked a cigarette. It was said that you can't embrace absolute good, unless you take in absolute evil. With that being said, Chris Bradley was the personification of that evil. On the surface, one would believe that he was a cop bent on solving crime, bringing criminals to justice, and ridding the city of drugs. However, Bradley was the complete opposite. Coming up in the streets of Delaware, he was fully aware of the wrong side of the tracks. His younger days of running with drug lords and gangsters showed him to use the streetwise sense more often and maneuver his way through.

His Irish and American heritage allowed him to have ties within the cartel section and with a few IRA and Mafia figures. He was the true friend of organized crime. Bradley knew the streets. He knew the criminals: how they walked, how they talked. He was a perfectionist, but he still had his own agenda. He was simply a criminal with a badge.

Having his hands dipped in the underworld was a way to flood the streets of Delaware with joy and fear. His seventy thousand dollar salary was nothing compared to what the dealers could make in a week. That was the true way for living the American dream.

When Bradley was up for promotion to chief of the homicide division, there was one person more qualified, and that was Detective Perkins. He was more of a show-off for the job. Not wanting to lose the lucrative and highly regarded position, Brad-ley hired the young hoodlum Cheek Raw. With Bradley's help, he located Perkins and executed him in front of his yard. After the murder of the detective went unsolved, Bradley made the spot and eventually lost it to investigations on tampering with evidence. Still, his reputation for getting things handled never failed. Cheek Raw was gonna be a witness to that.

* * *

Faith, West 5th Street

Ryan sat on the back porch of Faith's spot, soaking in the cool air. The full moon was sitting in the air, and the demons were definitely roaming for pleasure. What happened earlier with Cheek Raw placed his mind back to the negativity. A mother-fucker knew that messing with him was like jumping off Mount Everest. You would only get so far until you lost your life miser-ably.

As Wicked, Reckless, and DJ lounged around the crib, Faith stepped out of the glass sliding door, and closed it behind her. Folding her arms in the jacket, she moved over to him and sat in his lap.

"Why are you always trying to be alone, Ryan? We are still sitting in there waiting on you."

"I'm not trying to be alone. Sometimes I just like to mellow with no sounds. Out here is the best place," he said without taking his eyes from the moon.

"You know, I been thinking. I wanna name our baby Raekwon if it's a boy. If it's a girl, I would name her Kimyanna," Faith said ecstatically.

"I like that. I don't know about the boy name though. I don't need shit that's gonna remind me of that nigga." Ryan tapped his blunt.

"What do you mean? I thought you would love that idea for the baby. It'll be something to keep you closer to him."

Listening to the crickets sound off lightly in the breeze, he exhaled. "My dad didn't even want to be close to me when he was home. It's no point of me needing to latch onto him. He's gone. I loved him, but his heart showed me that my mom and I was only partially important. We didn't get that affection from him the way we should."

"Raekwon loved you, Ryan. I know that he didn't show it a lot. But this hood praises your name on the strength of him. I can see how they look at you when you walk around. Don't leave your father in the ground on a bad note."

"Why? What's the purpose if I don't even know who I'm try-ing to remember? My dad is the man who got my mother preg-nant. My entire life is based on stories and news clippings. He didn't leave me shit but a bad name. What else can I do besides live up to my last name?"

"I don't care what you think. Ever since I've been with you, we've been through stuff that could cause someone older than us to commit suicide. You're smart, and even if you were moving around with nothing, I would still feel the same way."

Markie D stepped out on the porch with a cup in his hand. "Baby girl. You mind if I holla at Ryan for a minute?

Faith rose to her feet and kissed his cheek. "I'll see you after y'all done."

"Okay."

As Faith made her way into the house, Markie-D came and took the seat next to Ryan.

"Wassup, young bull? I been trying to pull you over since ear-lier, but I don't want you to feel like I was killing yo' buzz."

"Nah, its' never no problem, Markie. I'm always open to hear-ing some good for me. I know it ain't no other way with you."

"Exactly. I really want you to know, man, that I'm ex-cited about my grandchild. At first I didn't approve because I didn't feel like y'all was prepared. It's not a toy. This is a child. I know that Faith loves you, and that's the reason I respect you enough to let this happen. I know you about yo' business, Ryan, but I really need you to tighten up now. My baby girl means the world to me. I know y'all gonna have differences also. It's the way life works. It's your job to keep it in order no matter what. This baby will bond you two forever."

"I'm not letting Faith go for anything. I know that a lot of people feel like we're gonna fail with this parent thing. But I'm positive that all will be well. I'm sure of it."

"How can you be sure? 'Cause that dope life ain't it. Trust me, Ryan. When I was your age, I shot every nigga I could. I tried to keep up with niggas like yo' dad. Out of all that shit, it didn't add up. The money disappeared and all those same niggas snitched on my ass when I got knocked for a murder charge. Nobody did a bitch-ass thing for me when I was caged in. It made me stronger. I knew that God existed when my lawyer got me off. I actually got the chance to make it back home to Faith and her mama. That's the reason I went off to the military. Be-cause it could only make me better for them. It's not about you no more when you build a family, young bull."

He sparked a the joint of marijuana and passed it to Ryan

"My point is, live for your family. We got a chance to be with our loved ones. Enjoy it. We can't rewind and re-verse this time, young blood. I would kill to see my friends again, to run with your dad and influence him to come back to school. We never got a chance to be kids because we were too busy being grown. You have a child coming, and I promise, you will get that same feel-ing, the feeling that what if I can't protect my baby? What if this lifestyle gets me killed? Ain't nobody about to care about that body count or that money when you riding in that hearse, fool. Be cautious. That's my only daughter. My only child. I don't want to lose her." Markie D looked directly in the eyes.

"I can't disagree with anything that you said. And you know I respect you to the utmost. I might not be shit to the next man, but I know you believe in me. So does Faith. That's the reason I'm sure about what I wanna do. I made my bed when me and her slept together with no protection. I've always loved her, and it will remain that way. As far as being in the streets, I can't just say that I will quit by tomorrow, but I'm damn sure not gon' think it'll last for-ever. If I step out here to get that bread, I'm going all the way. It's just the way I was brought up. My kid will be well-off. Faith is going to be well-off. So will you, because we're family now. I'm leading this throne regardless of who feels different, and there will be no exception. That's

the difference between me and my dad. I'm not giving niggas a chance to compete. Neither am I letting them slide
with anything. It's gonna be the one reason I survive until
I'm finished."

"That's respect, young bull. That's the reason I like
you. Plus I know that you can protect her. That's the way
it should be." Markie D shook Ryan's hand. "Remember
that being smarter gives you the advantage to avoid dumb
shit."

"Understood," Ryan said, gazing back at the moon.

The foundation was in process. Within the next few
months, Ryan was going to buy the city - either by choice
or force.

Chapter 13

Cheek Raw, New Castle, Delaware, 9:45 a.m.

"Yo, Sheen. Are you still pulling through or not?" Cheek asked while keeping an eye on Supreme's front door.

After finding out the hit was placed by Supreme, Cheek wasted no time sliding up for his revenge. It wasn't smart to waste time with a nigga so powerful. In order to show him that Cheek wasn't playing, he brought the business to his front door.

"So what's good, big bro? Is Sheen coming or not?" Balti-more asked with a sneaky grin.

"I don't know. All I'm waiting for is to see somebody. After that, we can take off with or without him." Cheek Raw clutched onto his Ruger P85 tightly.

"So is we taking it all or what? You know we can't come back if we do this."

Cheek thought about Baltimore's remark. He knew that shit could easily take a flip. Supreme was known to handle that issue, and if he didn't see you, then someone was going to come get you. Instead of being the hunted, Cheek would rather go all out to handle the pressure while it was in the air.

He spotted the white H-2 hummer that was pulling down. His heart rate increased.

"There she go." Baltimore nudged him. "Is we doing this or not?"

Taking a second to react, Cheek Raw cocked his gun as the Hummer came to a halt. Supreme's wife Franchesca stepped out. Cheek sprang into action. He and Baltimore jumped out of the car with their guns by their waists, speed walking over to her vehicle. She hopped out just as they reached her personal space.

"Don't move, bitch," Cheek hissed with his gun in her face.

All she could do was tremble. Her lips wanted to release a scream, but she didn't want to scare her daughter, who sat in the front seat. Baltimore quickly removed the young woman from the passenger seat. Smiling, Cheek led them towards the front door.

"Where is your husband?"

"I-I'm not sure. He left a few hours ago."

"Put the key in the door. Open it. If you obey, y'all will re-main safe."

Stepping up on the porch, she fumbled to unlock the door. After pushing it open, Cheek and Baltimore pushed the girls inside and locked up the home.

"Get in the living room and sit the fuck down. I don't wanna hurt y'all." Cheek waved his gun.

Following orders, Franchesca clutched onto her daughter and shifted through the home. The living room was quiet and Balti-more wasted no time rambling through the large crib.

Sitting on the opposite couch, Cheek Raw gazed at Francesca with a smirk. Her juicy breasts were bulging out for attention and her skintight jeans held a grip on her slim body. Her daughter was an exact replica of her. It like he was staring at Supreme's whole life in one room.

"You know that your husband is a very disrespectful man. That's the reason I'm here today."

"Me and my daughter have nothing to do with whatever my husband is mixed up in. You can deal with whatever you have to and we're not going to be in your way. There's money in the safe upstairs. You can have it all."

"Mom. Dad is gonna - "

"Hush. Just be quiet, Cynthia. I'm talking." Turning her atten-tion back to Cheek, Franchesca took a deep breath. "We have money upstairs. You can hurt me. Just leave my daughter out of this," Franchesca pleaded.

"Get up and come over here. Just you." Cheek held the gun by his side.

"It's okay." Francesca looked at her daughter before standing up. She moved over to him and stood directly in front of him.

"Get on your knees."

She did as she was told. She got down, positioning her-self right in front of him.

"How much you really love your daughter?" He rubbed the lining of her breast.

Wasting no time she unbuckled his belt. Before he could in-struct her, she took him down her mouth with ease. The sight of another man was well-needed, even with the danger that was occurring at the time. Supreme would only do so much when it came to pleasing her. The threat was more than a great opportuni-ty to release her feelings and save her family in the process.

Downing him quickly, she bobbed her head up and down. Her daughter looked on in amazement and crossed her legs. Pulling his cell phone out, Cheek started the video camera and watched as she swallowed him with passion. His mind didn't know if she was enjoying the moment, or if she was scared for her daughter's life. It truly didn't mat-ter.

"Mmm," she slightly moaned, not focused on the cam-era in front of her.

Cheek raised his vision up to Supreme's daughter. She quick-ly turned her head.

Cheek sent the short video to Supreme's phone. He took a few pictures and did the same. Franchesca was in her own world, and it surely wasn't by force.

* * *

Supreme, Eastside of Delaware, trap spot

"Hold on. Hold on. You said what?" Supreme listened close-ly to the news he was receiving.

"Yeah, man. Them niggas came through bussin', but they hit the wrong nigga. Cheek ain't fucking dead. The young bulls they killed were his workers. They were irrel-evant," the man spoke through the line.

"You mean to tell me out of three dead motherfuckers, none of those bodies is Cheek Raw?"

"Yeah, Severe didn't handle the business."

Feeling his anger elevate, Supreme bit his bottom lip. "Listen, you tell that fuck nigga Severe if this job wasn't handled and he took my money, we got a serious fucking problem!" Supreme barked loudly.

He heard the phone buzz, indicating a message. He pulled it away from his ear, clicking the multimedia mes-sage from Franchesca. The sight of her sucking another man's dick turned his stomach upside down. Before he could shout, more pictures began to fall in by the loads. The last picture of his daughter on her knees beside her pushed him over the limit.

"Tell Severe his ass is grass!" he yelled through the phone be-fore hanging up. He quickly called his wife, but received no answer, so he mashed the gas, heading for his home.

* * *

Supreme's home, Newcastle, Delaware

Arriving at home fifteen minutes later, Supreme jumped out of his truck and headed straight for the house. He never noticed the parked car sitting across from his spot. Muscling his way through the front door, he yelled his wife's name. "Franchesca!"

Before he could take another step, Baltimore's pistol crashed across his head. He fell to the floor and looked up at Cheek Raw coming down the stairs.

"If it ain't the big man. The nigga who sends hits instead of coming to do it himself."

The blurriness in his vision subsided before he glared up into his eyes. "I don't send hits, nigga. I been killing shit since you was in Pampers, young bull. If I had a problem, I would've been at you. "Supreme mugged him while holding the back of his head.

"That ain't what the streets talking, pussy. Niggas saying you giving out warnings. They should have warned yo' ass about me," Cheek said before releasing a shot in his arm.

Supreme groaned loudly, but tried his best to contain the screams like a real gangsta. Nothing was more horrible than letting another man seeing you beg like a bitch before you died, so he wasn't going out with that sad story.

"I fucked your wife and daughter. One of them might be pregnant. But don't worry. I didn't kill them. They just stuffed into the closet until we finished handling this business, boss."

"Fuck you, Cheek! It doesn't matter what you do. You can't hide that shit from Lil Raekwon forever. You think he ain't gon' find out?" Supreme shouted.

I don't know what the fuck you're talking about, nigga. Fuck Raekwon! Fuck you! Oh yeah. You can thank ya baby mama for giving me that code to your bank upstairs."

"Suck my dick, pussy!" Supreme spat a glob of blood on his shirt.

Pop! Pop! Pop! Pop! Pop! Cheek's gun unloaded with ease.

Fluttering his eyes back and forth, Supreme passed gas a few times before shitting his clothes.

"We need to get that safe down here!" Cheek looked over to Baltimore.

"It's not gon' fit, nigga. Just call Sheen. He has the truck. We can load it up in there and head back to the other side."

Glancing out of the window, Cheek called Sheen's line.

* * *

Sheen, Wilmington Delaware Police department, interrogation room 10:13 a.m.

"Listen to me you, little street punk. Your life is gonna be on the line for what you did. Ballistics came back with your name on that gun dropped behind the center. That weapon killed one of those victims. Maybe you were shooting with your eyes closed and made a mistake." Cross stared at him. He would blink every minute to make sure he caught any sign of guilt.

"I wasn't there on the shooting. Like the gun was in, like, the back of the center already. I just ran past 'cause I heard the gun."

Stepping over to Bradley, Cross whispered in his ear, "He's fucking lying.

"Oh, I'm pretty sure of that," he mumbled before walking over to Sheen. Taking a seat in front of him, he sparked a ciga-rette. "Look, kid, the season for beating murders is at a drought. I know you and Cheek Raw are running together. I hope you don't think that you're about to make it home to your little girlfriend like this."

Leaning his head down, Sheen nodded. "Y'all trying to get me murdered. Why can't you just go and ask him yourselves, man? I'm not trying to be mixed in no murder," he said with his hands on the table.

"Well, prove me wrong. Call him and set up the meeting." Bradley pulled out Sheen's phone, sliding it across the table to him. He tapped his finger.

Staring down at the touchscreen, Sheen huffed and picked it up. Before he could dial the number, Cheek Raw's name popped up on the front of his screen.

"Well I'll be damned. Pick it up." Cross pointed with a stern finger after spotting the caller.

Holding up a finger, Sheen answered and placed the line on speaker. "Wassup, li'l bro?"

"Where the hell are you?"

"Um, I'm on the block. Just chilling," he lied.

Bradley and Cross stood around listening to their wanted man speak through the phone.

"I need the truck. Pull up to Supreme's spot in Newcastle right now. We just struck good, nigga, so hurry up."

"Agree to it," Bradley whispered through clenched teeth.

"A'ight. I'm on the way now, bro. Sit still," Sheen re-plied be-fore hanging up.

Wasting no time, Bradley jumped on his walkie talkie. "This is Detective Bradley to dispatcher. I need a team of men out in Newcastle right now en route for a suspect. Highly dangerous. May be armed!"

"Roger that, Bradley. Dispatch out," the voice sounded off a few seconds after.

"Keep him here. I'll go and handle this with Cheek. I waited months to see this bitch go down." Bradley snatched Sheen's phone back before running out the door.

Chapter 14

Scrambling through the crib, gathering everything they could, Cheek Raw and his accomplice Baltimore prepared themselves for the celebration. After Supreme was removed from his space, it would leave the doors open for anyone to grab. He was the glue inside of Delaware.

Stepping in front of the window, Baltimore glanced out at the S.W.A.T. cars that were sliding in front of the house.

"Cops!" he yelled, alerting Cheek.

Running back downstairs, they glanced out the window at all the police units.

"Shit!" Cheek Raw hit the wall with his fist.

* * *

"Move! Move! Move!" Bradley shouted as his unit exited their vehicles, surrounding the block. They made sure to cover their tracks on any suspects cruising away from the scene. The police officials, armed with M16 assault rifles, moved swiftly to set a perimeter around the house.

A bundle of bullets released out of the front door. Sheltering behind their cars.They aimed their weapons just in case someone came out with their bullets blazing.

olding his handgun, Bradley grabbed the megaphone and spoke inside. "We have the house surrounded .Come out with your hands up, Cheek Raw. We know you're in there. Make it easy on yourself."

"I got a hostage. Step the fuck back!" he yelled through the door.

Waving his hand, Cross called Bradley over to the sideline. "You know that we can't go in there if he has hostages, right? How the hell are you gonna pull this off?"

"He's coming out, or I'm coming in." Bradley took of this jacket.

* * *

Cheek held his gun in hand as he watched the officers move around sneakily.

"Want the fuck we gon' do, bro? I told you I can't take no bid," Baltimore complained with his gun aimed for the front door. "We gotta be a man about this shit. I'll take the armed robbery, but I ain't claiming no murder."

"What! Nigga, we on this move together. What the fuck are you talking about? You in on this money, ain't you?" Cheek's face balled up with anger.

"Yeah, but we ain't about to keep this money, Cheek. Look out there, man. This shit over with!" He pointed at all the flashing lights outside.

Grabbing the side of his head in aggravation, Cheek raised his pistol to Baltimore's head and pulled the trigger.

Boc!

The gunshot caused the police to shuffle around the front yard. If Cheek was going down, it surely wasn't going to be with a codefendant. Baltimore's words didn't match his actions and the statements he made gave a clear indication that he was going to tell the judge everything.

"Come out with your hands up. We will come in to get you," Cross's voice sounded off through the megaphone.

Pacing back and forth in a circle. Cheek thought about using the wife and daughter. If a slug to one of their head didn't scare them, then he was willing to take his chances on running. Dying wasn't a fucking option, and there was no way that he could run off without his back being filled with bullets.

Before he could make his next move, Bradley came around the corner of the wall with his pistol aimed at Cheek Raw's head. "I'll knock yo' shit right off ya damn head, boy. Put it down! Now!" he shouted with major aggression.

Looking at Bradley in his eyes, Cheek threw down the weap-on. "So I guess you made it your business to see me, huh?"

"Naw, I'm not, but that cold-ass jail cell is waiting for you, Raw. I told you that I would catch you, didn't I? You fucked yo' life up, and now you've killed an innocent man." Bradley nodded his head towards Supreme, whose body rested on the living room floor.

"What's next, Bradley? I got out before. I'll get out again. Me and you know what I know."

Stepping over to him, he placed him into handcuffs and smiled. "See, that's the difference, Raw. It's my word against yours. You're sitting in a house with two bodies, maybe more. Your testimony will be like a bitch who's late on paying big daddy, you little faggot."

"We'll see about that." Cheek smirked.

"Dispatcher. Suspect is secured and in custody. Send the units in," he radioed on his walkie talkie. "Guess what, Raw? I know what you think, but it's not gonna work. I'm so glad Sheen was with us when you needed that truck. We would've never known."

Hearing Sheen's name his expression quickly change.

"That's right, motherfucker. Game over," Bradley whispered into his ear before the cops swarmed the entire home.

* * *

Ryan's spot, 8th and Adams

Shaking Ryan out of his sleep, Faith pulled him out of the bed.

"Girl, what the hell are you doing? I'm asleep."

"Ryan, come look at this."

Grabbing his hand, she pulled him to the living room, where DJ and Rose sat on the couch. The TV was extra loud and it was the news broadcasting the live footage down in Newcastle.

"Look," Faith pointed. "They found Cheek."

Walking over by the flat screen, Ryan looked at the police brining Cheek Raw out of a suburban home. His face was low-ered before they placed him in the back of a police car. The subtitle read: Murderer caught red-handed.

Shaking his head, DJ stood up. "Bro, that's right down the street from my new spot.

"I gotta find out what the fuck is going on." Ryan grabbed his cell phone.

"Baby wait. I don't think that might be a good idea to call anyone concerning him. Those weren't regular cops. They wore SWAT vests and badges, which means the feds could get in-volved."

"She right." DJ followed up. "This shit might cause a lot of niggas to get booked. I been in a couple of places with this man, and ain't no telling what a nigga say when them folks get ahold of him."

"Hell naw! Cheeks ain't doing no ratting. I don't give a fuck what nobody say. It's no telling how he got tied into this shit. Just because he get knocked don't mean that we can bash his name that he might tell on us," Ryan said.

"That's not the point, bro. If he's hot, then anyone associated with him is being watched. You're staying in this nigga's crib. How we know these folks ain't gon' run up in this bitch any second now? Trust me, bro. We need to relocate."

"If this shit is gonna mess up anything dealing with our child, I'm snapping." Faith was starting to show and her emotions were pushing the dash for the past few days.

"Just calm down. All I'm gonna do is flip out and lose it. I'm trying to think, if you would just shut the fuck up, Faith." Ryan was moving too fast, and the news threw him into a dysfunction-al state.

"Listen, you and Rose need to go to the house. I don't need you around this hot-ass apartment. I barely got enough energy on dealing with your mama. She's not about to kill me because of you getting twisted in some shit that you got nothing to do with.

"Fuck Cheek! He ain't got nothing to do with us. I say ditch this shit and stay the hell out of those streets, Ryan. This stuff is going too far. The next thing we gon' see is you being taken away in cuffs. We can all go." Faith rolled her neck.

"You're being overrated right now. Take yo' ass home, and I'm gon' hit you back when I'm coming to get you." He kissed her.

"Uh, y'all do know that Cheek knows where we all live," Rose reminded them.

"I don't care what that nigga knows. We ain't got nothing to do with him getting knocked. If he sends them folks our way, I'll get his ass bodied in prison. Until then, head home and we meet back later on tomorrow."

"Fine." Faith grabbed her purse and car keys before walking out with Rose behind her.

"Bruh. This might be bigger than us, Ryan. You know niggas asses get what they looking for when you go snooping for the trouble. If we don't know what's going on, it might be safer for us to leave this alone," DJ said with his hands moving back and forth.

"You ain't gotta worry. All I'm doing is pushing up on this man's associates. I still haven't met this plug yet. Cheek owes me. I don't give a fuck if the Navy SEAL's came to scoop that nigga up. We had a deal, and that was to give me the way. I'll link up with you after I do my own research." Ryan grabbed his coat to leave.

Tuning back in to the news footage, DJ shook his head. If Cheek Raw was being arrested on murder charges, someone was playing foul. It was known to work like that in the streets of Wilmington. The only scary thing about it was the surprise. You never knew who was out to get you. You could run and hide, but what happened if that surprise backstabber was standing directly next to you?

Chapter 15

Sheen, 7th and Montgomery

Pushing his whip down the filthy neighborhood, Ryan pon-dered on his luck. Just when it was time for his come up, it was squandered by the actions of some bullshit. Cheek Raw getting knocked cut the chances for a nigga to even think about getting a brick of dope .Supreme was the next in line, and according to the news special, he wouldn't be serving anybody for a very long time.

Sliding down to the bottom of 7th, he spotted Sheen stepping out of his front door. Busting a U-turn, he swerved inside of the parking lot and pulled next to him. "Sheen?"

"Wassup, who that?" He jumped like a deer in the head-lights.

"Nigga, it's me. Ryan."

Lowering his head to look inside of the Infiniti truck, Sheen stepped closer. "Ryan? Damn, dawg. You can't sneak up on a nigga like that." Sheen carried two huge black bags in his hands, and his head was pouring beads of sweat.

"What happened to Cheek?"

"Man, this shit is ugly, Ryan. I don't know who to trust. They knocking the homies off day by day. Word is that Cheek bodied this nigga Supreme. Everybody is in a ram-page. Niggas saying that Cheek might fuck around and snitch." Sheen stuttered.

"What the fuck make you say some shit like that? You don't know what the fuck he gon' do," Ryan said with an offended expression.

"Ryan, wake up, young bull. Cheek has crossed the en-tire Wilmington out for scraps and packs. How do you think he came up so well? It's bad blood out here and I'm not about to be in the middle."

Looking at the packed bags, Ryan raised his eyebrow. "I take it that you going on vacation."

Shuffling in his shoes, Sheen stumbled over his words. "Nah. I'm... I just gotta get the hell out of here, young bull. I'm not trusting nothing right now at this time."

Ryan watched him throw the bags in the back of his girl's car. He got in the driver's seat. Glancing at the license plate, Ryan logged it into his memory before Sheen skated off.

* * *

Reckless, 10:00 p.m., abandoned building outside of Wilmington

Reckless pulled up next to the parked car. Stepping put, he eyed Sheen, who sat on the top of his car hood.

"You late. I been waiting for you two hours, Reckless."

"Relax, nigga. You act like a nigga trying to finesse you or some, bruh. Chill the fuck out."

"Relax! Nigga, Cheek is gone. We had a deal. I did my part and got him out of the way. You didn't know that I was snatched up by the narcs this morning? They wanted Cheek so bad that they pressed me to call and set him up. Pay me, Reck-less."

"The narcs snatched you up this morning? What all did you say?"

"I told them what I needed to for Cheek to be removed. That's all," Sheen said as he cast his eyes down to the concrete.

"Mmm. Cool. Go ahead and grab the money out the trunk." Reckless looked out at the streets as if someone was watching them.

"Cool." Moving towards the car, Sheen pressed the button to open the trunk, making his way to the back. He opened the black bag that sat in the inside.

As he slid the zipper down, Reckless placed a bullet into his brain.

Boc!

Before his body could crumble, he grabbed Sheen by his armpits and tossed him inside, slamming the trunk down. He stood back for a second to catch a deep breath. Nothing was more vicious than a man who could get you knocked by the police. He wasn't taking chances with being locked away, nor was he trying to be seen. Still and all, it was in Reckless's plan. Everybody was walking around like Ryan was god. The weak-ass favoritism from Cheek Raw was cutting holes into their pockets. In order to beat the best, you either join them, or eliminate the rest.

Jumping back into the rental, Reckless smiled and drove off slowly with Sheen's body simmering inside the trunk.

* * *

Ryan, 8:35 a.m., 8th and Adams

Feeling his phone vibrate numerous times, Ryan snapped his eyes open to search for it, tossing the sheets and blanket around. It fell against the floor.

Picking it up, he answered, "Yo?"

"Don't say no names, and listen to me clear, li'l bro," Cheek said through the line.

"What's good, bro? I heard about what happened. Are you good, nigga?"

"Yeah, listen. This was my last strike, li'l bro. I've been back and forth in this shit fourteen times. These people are about to hang me from a tree. This might sound crazy, but I knew that it was coming. That nigga Sheen…handle that. He snitched on me, li'l bro."

"What! I just saw that nigga yesterday. He was acting all nervous and shit. The nigga packed some bags and said that you was probably about to turn state. He peeled out." Ryan jumped out of his bed enraged.

"Damn! That bitch did me down bad. I'm waiting on these pussy-ass cops to come see me. It's not too much that I can really say, li'l bro. You have to be careful with the people who around you out there. I got a lot of enemies, and they gon' be feeling some type of way about you being my young bull."

"Fuck these niggas. You know I can handle my own. I'm just not looking for any trouble. I'm moving straight and I'm damn sure not about to get off course for the miscellaneous shit."

"Always." Cheek laughed. "Check this. I want you to go and check my laundry room, right? Lift up that clothes hamper. 2112 is the code. Put half on my jail account and keep the rest of it."

"Word, man, is there anything I can do? I can get at some of yo' people and make them come in until we find Sheen."

"No need. He's gonna be found sooner or later. It doesn't matter what he do. My name is stamped on that turf for a reason, young bull. You know that I would never say yo' name dealing with anything. So if a nigga disrespect my honor, handle him smoothly."

"Understood."

"Listen, I'll call you tomorrow and let you know what else I'm trying to handle. Keep ya eyes open."

"Always," Ryan stated before hanging up.

The news about Sheen was accurate, just as he suspected. A nigga's movements never lied, and yesterday Ryan witnessed the betrayal in his eyes. A snake always happened to slither through the cracks. There was only one way to wash them out.

Heading to the bathroom, he spotted the old hamper sitting in the corner. Moving it to the side, Ryan stared at the small square mounted into the floor. Opening it up, it revealed a stainless steel chrome safe. Bending down to the floor, he stared in amazement. During the few months he resided in Cheek's apartment, Ryan never noticed that he was sitting around a large check the entire time.

After typing in the four digit code, he opened the safe's door.

"Damn!" He glared at the folded rubber band banks.

He removed the cash and spotted a black business card that rested underneath the dead presidents. He picked it up and stared at the letters M.C. with an address at the bottom. The texture of the card was smooth with gold trimmings. Shrugging his shoul-ders, he tossed it into the bag with the cash. Wrapping it up, he headed back for the living room.

After evaluating the situation, Ryan made up the decision to get his own spot. After tomorrow, things were changing. No one would be able to pinpoint his whereabouts. The hunt for Sheen was on, and nobody was gonna stop him from taking the streets by the throat.

* * *

Demerea's house,11:34 a.m.

"Girl, Cheek Raw ain't no valuable nigga in my eyes, Faith. He's been around here putting the press on the hood like he a muthafucking Prince. Fuck him," Demerea said with anger.

She was tired of talking about the bum Cheek Raw. Ever since Faith heard the news, she was in more of a panic than anyone else. The thought of Ryan fucking her a few days ago was steaming hard. It was never her intention to hurt the girl who she considered to be her best friend. Nothing was like a man who could hold a secret. The deceit between her and Ryan was at an all-time high. After giving him the good head that he deserved, he was hooked ever since. That was just the normal way of a great freak.

Smiling with a sneaky smile, she looked over at Faith. Her stomach was protruding more by the day, and it was a blessing to be pregnant by the next big man of the city.

"What about Ryan, Faith? How could you sit here and keep thinking about Cheek when your man is following in his same footsteps? We both know how it goes in Delaware. You earn your name, and eventually someone takes it, whether it's a street nigga or the feds. Ryan's name has been ringing bells out here ever since his father left. You have to know that the same thing is about to happen with him." Demerea threw slight shade.

"I mean, I have trust in Ryan, girl. I know he loves me and our baby. All I'm trying to do is get him to see that. He's not gonna make the same mistakes. He knows that we have a family now."

"Family," Demerea repeated. "Bitch, that nigga ain't worried about nobody but DJ. He's with them more than you. Look, you aren't even at school today. This is the last few months before we graduate, and he hasn't shown you any support. He dropped out, and now he throwing his dirty plans into your brain. Don't make the wrong decision and end up in a jail cell beside this man. Think about what your mama would say. You have to focus on that child because his rampage has just begun."

.Faith thought about the drama that Ryan was causing. Even her father Markie-D gave her advice about settling for a young bull who was stuck in the criminal mind frame. The police would have no compassion, and that would leave their child's father either in prison or a graveyard.

"You right. I'm thinking about dropping this baby right now. After that's done, if he still want to be a part of Delaware's most wanted list, he'll be eating alone in his cell. Of course, my mama put me on game. She doesn't even like Ryan. But it's nobody's decision but mines if I choose to stand by him. Just support me. If he's gonna stop, he'll do it before this child is birthed."

Demerea smirked at her remark. She knew one thing for sure. From the color of her bomb skin to the powerful mouth game, she was one that a man couldn't resist. Ryan would be hers if Faith didn't put the foot down soon enough. It took a real woman to nurture a killer, and her best friend just wasn't fit. If only she knew that slime game that was about to be formatted, she would slide her baby out five months early and take off to another country.

"I guess. Maybe he will come around?" Demerea said before focusing on the movie in front of them.

Hearing the doorbell ring, Demerea jumped to her feet. "I got it."

Walking out of the living room, she made the sharp turn and opened it.

Reckless stood with his hands folded while leaning back on the guard rail. His face stated that he was aggravated, and that was the last thing Demerea needed.

"What are you doing here?" she whispered, stepping outside of the home to close the door.

"I'm on a mission right now. You remember what we were talking about the other day?" he asked.

"Yeah, why?"

"Because it's about that time. I know you got your own little tricks up your sleeve also, but don't forget the objective."

"You don't have to remind me, Reckless. Faith is sitting in-side the house. What is it that you want me to do?

"Sell my car. Whatever you make off of it, you keep."

Giving him a funny look, she stared at the vehicle sitting in her yard. "Why? What did you do?"

"Nothing major. Just handle it."

Chapter 16

Cheek Raw, 1:25 p.m., Wilmington holding facility

Hearing the buzzer to his cell door, Cheek heard the guard yell his name for an attorney visit. He got out of his bed, tossed on his T-shirt, and headed out of to the multi-purpose area. Walking go the small flight of steps. He stepped inside the visita-tion booth, and closed the door behind him, waiting patiently for his lawyer. He leaned back.

The expression on his face showed the anger as Detective Bradley walked through the other side with a smile.

"Mr. Ass Cheeks, how you doing, baby?" He sat down in the chair.

Balling up his face, Cheek Raw picked up the wall phone. "You got a lot of nuts coming up here, Bradley!"

"Aww, man. Come on, bro. I thought we were partners?"

"We ain't shit. You could have turned your head and let me make it out of that shit. After all the fucking money I gave you, nigga? Not one time have I ever crossed you out."

Slanting his eyes, Bradley spoke smoothly into the phone. "Calm the fuck down. Who are you trying to alert, Raw? We're having a grown man conversation, so lower your voice. I've stood beside you when your pockets were in a coma. You didn't listen, and now when you fall down, it's everyone's fault besides yours, right? Before you answer that, remember who you're talking to, buddy," Bradley warned with a pointed finger.

"I'm sitting in a cell right now. These people ain't letting me out of here no time soon. I been twisted in the system for years, Bradley. How can you lock the nigga up who paying you double times your salary, stupid mother-fucker? I've killed niggas and saved your ass, if you don't remember. But I guess we can't speak on that, huh?" Cheek leaned back in seat.

Chuckling, Bradley scooted closer to the window. "Let me make you aware you of something. I still have a job to do. Noth-ing will get in the way of that, and I'm surely not failing 'cause you wanna play the assassin of Wilmington, idiot. You've had the chance to put this city in a chokehold, but instead, you slipped. I see your little protégé is up and running. Seems like he got the same nuts as his father."

"You mean because you scared of his pops, right?" Cheek laughed. "Come on, Bradley. Raekwon put the press on the entire police force, and you was in the same bunch. Now that he's gone., you've turned into a full-fledged mercenary nigga. Remind me... Did you have Raekwon under extortion, or did he have you under protection.

"Fuck Raekwon! You thought that he was gon' last forever, nigga? You talkin' about the same man who was stabbed to death in his cell. Gutted like a fish on dry land. I'ma explain something to you. punk. My connections will reach so far to touch you. I'll strive night and day to make sure you receive the dirtiest fate ever. You think that you have something over my head? That doesn't even add up to half of the things I can place on you, Cheek. The murders, the drugs... I'm not even done, bastard. There's a list in my pocket that I can pull out. It's long enough to stretch from here to Philly. Now let's get this cleared up. You owe me money, Cheek, and I want it." Bradley paused to see if he would speak.

"Nigga, I'm in here. How the fuck am I gon' give you any-thing? I'm having to buy lawyers and other shit in order to get a number on a plea. You pressing me now!

"You have assets, Raw. As I said, your little follower is mak-ing a name for himself. Address him to get his mind correct, and maybe we can have you out of here in twenty years."

Shaking his head, Cheek turned his face away from the glass for a slight second. "What type of deal is that? In twenty years, I'll be fifty, motherfucker."

"Or you can take the four life sentences they're about to offer you and live happily ever after.

Looking down at the table, tapping his finger repeatedly, Cheek thought about the proposition. "This ain't nothing that you can guarantee me. Is you running your mouth, Bradley?

Getting to his feet, he grinned. "That's the difference about me. I have no reason to play when I'm in charge. I truly under-stand why they call you Cheek. You're a real asshole.

Turning on his heels, Bradley left the visitation booth.

The only thing that Cheek was thinking about was Ryan. He didn't want to send Bradley his way, but four life sentences was something that he couldn't stomach. If it meant having the young one to work off his situation, he would just have to make that sacrifice.

* * *

Ryan, 7th and Montgomery, 7:45 p.m.

After leaving the nearest burger shack, Ryan cruised down the block to see if he could catch a glimpse of the slimeball Sheen. His mind was still spinning from the snitching shit. That's why he made it his business to place a bullet in the rat's head.

Rotating his eyes back and forth, he jumped after the police sirens sounded off. The unmarked car caused him to fumble with his gun. He slid it under his shirt, slowed down, and pulled to the side.

He watched the cop step out of his car, gun in hand. Ryan pre-pared to pop some shit if necessary. The handle of the officer's gun tapped lightly against the window.

Ryan rolled it down and stared up into Bradley's eyes. "Is there a problem, sir?

"Yeah, as a matter of fact there is, Ryan."

"How do you know my name?" He mugged up and down at the man. Niggas was willing to do whatever to get a top don murdered. Slipping was not about to be sweet on that end, even if he had to take the hard route out.

"Let's just say Cheek Raw blessed me to be in your presence, Mr. Wilmington. I heard great things about you, and now it seems like we are finally able to cross paths.

"No one can bless you on meeting me. He ain't never said nothing about no cop!" Ryan spat. "If I'm not being arrested for anything, you need to back up from my whip."

Laughing, Bradley leaned down into the window. "Guess what? Without me, there would've been no Cheek Raw. So now I'll tell you what. Every week, I want ten grand. Every week. If you miss a payment, your ass will be in jail before you make your weekly re-up. Do I make my-self clear?" Bradley stood with a hand on his gun.

Nodding, Ryan rolled up his window and slowly pulled away. As his car slid out into traffic, he smiled. Money was the reason he got out to protect the community. Nothing was going around him, and Ryan was the next person on list.

* * *

Precious

After pulling down on 8th and Adams, Precious turned into Ryan's spot and cut off her engine, then stepped out. She sported a pair of tight sweatpants and a Nike tennis shirt. Her hair was wrapped in a ponytail, as usual, and the order of fish and fries lingered through the air as she headed to his door.

She knocked lightly and waited. Her eyes would look at her surroundings every few seconds to make sure that she wasn't running into any trouble. She heard the locks shift. Ryan opened the door and smiled at the sight of her beauty.

"Hey Ryan."

"What's good, ma? Come in." He stepped to the side, allow-ing her to enter.

"I brought us something to eat while we talk. I don't know if you like fish or not, but my mom's catering service is the absolute truth." She smiled, setting the bags on his coffee table.

"Your mom owns a catering service?"

"Yes. She has for the past twenty years," Precious nodded.

Digging in her pocket, she pulled out a white envelope and handed it to him. "Here's the money that you gave me to invest, plus what you made."

Opening it, Ryan fingered through the bills like an expert. "Girl, this is like fifteen thousand dollars. What the hell did you invest into, dope?

Laughing, Precious sat down at the table and grabbed her cell phone. "No, silly, stocks and bonds."

"Stocks and who? What the hell is that? You know I'm a street dude. I can't speak that college lingo. English, please." He sat down next to her.

"That is crazy. Stocks and bonds. It's a certain amount of money that you can put into a company, like a form of investing, except you're watching the market scale constantly to see whose business is going down or up. It helps you to invest in the right thing and gain your money back. Maybe even triple it. You just gotta have an eye for it."

"So you made fifteen thousand dollars by giving somebody else yo' money?" Ryan asked, confused.

"Yes. I know it may sound crazy, but this is why I wanted to start sitting down with you. If I can map out a game plan to teach you about business, you can master little steps like stocks and bonds in no time. That's just a small stage. It eventually leads to property, clothing shops, or franchises. Once you learn how to invest, your money will recycle itself.

Ryan stared at her while she spoke. He became lost in her beauty. Her perfect teeth and beautiful smile added on to the sight. She was highly intelligent, which was a major turn on. You could rarely discover a woman who knew how to do a man's job better than he could. She was truly a winner. Precious was the bright side of a wonderful future, and Ryan could smell it a mile away.

"So what is it that you wanna do? Since you like to invest, what do you think we can accomplish together? Something that could be profitable for the both of us?"

"Well, for the past six months, I've been developing a market-ing plan for a club. I think that with the right property and the right location, it could be great. I always wanted to be like a promoter. Sometimes my mom tells me that I'm moving too fast, but I can't help the dream that I see. She wants me to follow behind her with the catering business. That's not my dream though." Precious shook her head.

"So how much do you think that it'll take to build this club. What all will it take?" Ryan scooted closer to her

"Uh, my limit was a hundred thousand. I know that it might take about six months to construct it all. I can start off with fifty and work my way to the top. I've planned this for the longest. It's no way that I'm failing, no matter how long it takes. I was thinking about taking out a loan."

Rising to his feet, Ryan pulled a bag out from the side of his sofa. He removed the money that she requested. He handed her $35,000 and placed the envelope back into her palms. "I see that I can trust you, and I like that. You didn't have to bring me anything back off that money, but you did. I would love to give you the money to start this dream off for you. Who knows how far it can go?" Ryan took his seat back next to her.

"Why would you do that for me?" She gazed into his eyes.

"Why would you bring me back fifty thousand dollars?

"Because, it was your money, Ryan." She crossed her legs.

"Well, I guess you answered your own question." He smiled, pinching her cheek.

Smiling, she placed a quick kiss on his lips. "This is something you won't regret. I can guarantee you a successful business within six months. Do you have a name in mind?"

"What about Club Royal?"

"I like that," Precious said, jotting it down in her phone. "Club Royal it is."

"A'ight, enough about work. We supposed to be thirty minutes into this movie by now." Ryan placed the Netflix channel on his television.

After setting the mood, he killed the lights and sat back down. Precious wasted no time snuggling up under him.

"Ryan, why do you stay in the streets so much? You're so smart. Like I've never been around a person who's confident about another's dream. I know there has to be something you want to do on your own?" she asked while staring at the TV.

Shaking his head, he smirked. "It's only a few things that I'm good at. I've never put my mind to thinking of anything beyond Delaware. That's the reason I respect your mind so much. You show me that there may be a chance to do something different. Maybe I'll do a clothing line or something. I've always had a thing for fashion."

"I'll stand behind you," she assured him with a warm smile.

Gazing down at her gorgeous face, Ryan felt her sincerity. Not everyone was reliable enough to put your trust and time into them. Precious was different. She wasn't for self, nor did she have a savage bitch's ways. Her mind was green to the fast life, and that's where Ryan wanted to keep her. Not only would she be a great business partner, but she could potentially be a long-term friend. That was all he needed at the time. Respect and loyalty.

Chapter 17

Tyleema's house, Newark, Delaware,11:42 p.m.

"At the end of the day, if we can pull this off, we will be straight for good. That's the reason we have to do our homework thoroughly. Nothing is guaranteed to go right when we freestyle shit," Tyleema said as Wicked and Reckless sat at the kitchen table.

"So how long are you supposed to do this homework? Be-cause it's a limit. I'm not trying to be doing too much studying. We rob for a living. Remember?

"That's besides the point. This isn't the ordinary move that y'all are used to pulling. It's a small gambling house in the basement. This nigga has security and all. The whole nine."

"All we have to do is get Ryan over here to think of a solid plan," Sekoya suggested.

"Ryan?" Reckless screwed up his face. "He ain't got nothing to do with this move. He's a trapper now - or you must forgot?"

"Yeah, but he also said that if it's worth it, he's willing to make an exception. If I say he's a part of it, he's a part of it," she replied

"Are you crazy? You think you can just put this nigga in our place on making the shit happen? I'm tired of even hearing this man's name. Fuck all that, bitch! If I say that nigga ain't in, then that's final. We the ones going in here to lay these motherfuckers down. Nobody else."

"Bitch? Nigga, who the fuck you talking to? I don't give a damn what you think you about to do.This is my move, not Tyleema's. Not Teona's. Mine. If I want him to be a part of this, he's in."

"Sekoya, calm down. You don't have to do all that about this boy. When we started doing this, we said that we would work together. You can't get mad at how they feel. Ryan is a little too much, in my opinion," Tyleema replied.

"What? Ryan has helped with everything we done. Most of those robberies would have went totally different if he wasn't there. I'm not talking up for anybody. He's a valuable asset to this team."

Reckless pulled out his gun and pulled the hammer back swiftly. Walking over to Sekoya, he grabbed her by the hair and placed the gun to her chin. "Maybe I gotta explain to you what the fuck I do. Blowing muthafucka's brains out is my specialty," he whispered in her ear.

"Get the fuck off me," she whimpered, feeling the cold steel against her skin.

"Reckless, chill the fuck out. Don't do that shit." Wicked rose out of his chair.

Tyleema's scary ass couldn't do anything but watch in fear. After having the same recent encounter with Reckless a few days prior, she knew that there was no debating with him.

"You better tighten up, Sekoya. If you on that nigga's side, then you against me. He's not a part of this move. Simple. As long as you agree, we will be okay. Now do we have an under-standing?" His lips were close to her ear.

"Yeah."

Pushing her head, he then turned around to face Tyleema and Wicked. "That goes for everybody. Our business is our business. Ryan sells dope. He doesn't rob. Leave that to us, and let's get this money." He took a seat back in his chair.

Huffing with anger, Sekoya grabbed her coat and stepped outside on the porch. Holding her phone in hand, she dialed Ryan's number. She headed down the steps to get a small dis-tance away from the house.

She heard his voice speak through the line. His voice was groggy, as if he just rolled out of the bed. "What's up, Sekoya?"

"Ryan…" She sniffled as tears came to her eyes.

"What happened? Are you okay?" He sat up in his bed.

"I need to talk to you."

"Come over. I'll get up"

After hanging up, she climbed into her car and pulled off.

* * *

DJ, Ryan's spot, 8th and Adams

"This is the reason I told you to ditch them niggas, bro. Reck-less is corrupted, and Wicked gonna follow suit because that's his family. If one is slime, both are slime. That's the way I feel," DJ spat.

"It's Tyleema too. She's my friend, but Reckless has some type of spell over this hoe. She jumps when this man says move. She don't want anybody else to be a part of the licks but Reck-less and Wicked. I don't think we should trust her ass either," Sekoya spat.

"So you telling me that this nigga pulled a gun out on you, and Wicked didn't stop this man?" Ryan asked.

He was quite sick of Reckless. His envious-ass behavior was becoming overbearing, and now it felt as if he was ready to pump his nuts up for a beef. He only felt like he was a killer. Nothing would stop Ryan from blowing out his brains if he even thought about pulling another disrespectful action.

"No, they just sat there and watched. He has it out for you. I don't know what personal beef y'all got going on, but Reckless gets furious every time your name is said." Sekoya shook her head.

"I say we just continue on with our movement and cut them folks off. Ain't no way we about to have a successful operation if Reckless and Wicked moving around on some sneaky shit. It's like a war between family happening on the low," DJ stressed.

"Fuck it. I'll just pull up on both of them niggas today and see if they ready to die together. I don't have time to look behind me, and I refuse to see any one of mines get hurt."

"No, trust me, bro. Have patience. We need to get you out of this crib, first of all. After that, whatever you want to do, I'm with it," DJ suggested.

"I don't know what they have planned, so you might wanna move fast. They trying to hit this lick and come for your spot." Sekoya stood up with her arms folded.

"A lick can't help them niggas touch me. A li'l hundred thou-sand ain't about to do it," Ryan stated arrogantly.

"This ain't that type of move, Ryan."

"What do you mean? What is it?"

"A million dollars," she said seriously.

* * *

Four months later

Cheek Raw's murder trial

The atmosphere of the courtroom was so dull. The faces in the jurors' section looked as if they were ready to give away all the time God could offer, and the judge stared at Cheek Raw like he killed his wife, who had died from cancer three years prior.

"Your Honor, I've been sitting up here for the past two hours and explained to the people and citizens of this courtroom about what we're dealing with. My patience has run thin with Mr. Rodgers. This name he goes by on the street, 'Cheek Raw'...it's a disgrace. He's murdered many people in Wilmington ever since he was released from his last conviction. This man is a full-fledged criminal and I'm here to make sure that he never sees daylight again. Now I don't know if the people are okay with murderers running around their neighborhood. Wilmington is only so big. What if one of our kids is next? Or maybe even our wives? We can't show this animal mercy for the crimes that he has committed. The State rests," District Attorney Kelly said.

Cheek Raw's attorney spoke next. "The Defense calls Detec-tive Bradley."

Detective Bradley got up from his seat and moved towards the front.

The bailiff approached him with a fresh Holy Bible. "Place your right hand on the book and raise your right hand."

Detective Bradley did as he was told. He stared over at Cheek, who was mugging him.

Detective Bradley sent him a slight smile. He swore to tell the whole truth and nothing but the truth. Of course, it was permissi-ble for him to break the rules a little.

"Detective Bradley, can you explain to us what happened the day you arrested my client?"

"Well, I arrested one of his formal associates, who goes by the name Sheen. He was drug peddler, a small dealer who kissed ass to please Cheek Raw. After investigating the triple homicide on 5th and Madison, we discovered a handgun behind the recrea-tional center.I sent it in to ballistics, and forensics retrieved the fingerprint, which is how I located Sheen Watson. The only strange thing about this situation was that Watson's gun was never fired. It let me known that this was more of a professional on the scene: your one and only Cheek Raw."

"Motherfucker, you dead!" Cheek spat while hopping up from his seat.

"Mr. Rodgers, one more outburst like that and you'll be charged with terroristic threats against a police officer and I will send you back to the facility. Detective Bradley, please finish," Judge Patterson ordered.

"Of course. As I said, after finding the prints, I located Mr. Watson in front of a liquor store. After taking him in for ques-tionin, he admitted that Cheek Raw was the shooter who created the gun battle. In the middle of interrogation, he received a call from Raw asking to come down to Newcastle, which is where we found him - at the victim's house, red-handed." He cut his eyes over to the district attorney.

"So did you actually see my client murder these people?" Cheek's lawyer asked.

"No, but I'm quite sure that he did it. He was the only one alive. Even his accomplice was murdered after the fact. We heard gunshots while standing in front of the home. After that, I took it upon myself to make my way inside through a window to subdue the suspect."

"The defense rests."

* * *

After clearing his throat, Judge Patterson shuffled through his papers. "Jurors, are we ready for the verdict?

The white jury foreman rose to his feet. He nodded. "Alex-ander Rodgers, we the jury find you guilty of all charges."

Cheek grabbed the collar of his lawyer's suit and pulled him close. No one could understand what he was saying, but judging from the look on his face, it was nothing nice.

"Mr. Rodgers, I hope that you learn a lesson with your life in prison. I sentence you to serve three life sentences to be served consecutively. May God have mercy on you, Sir." The judge slammed the gavel.

The verdict caused Cheek Raw's stomach to cave in. Detec-tive Bradley had committed the ultimate betrayal, and so did his partner in crime, Detective Cross. Cheek turned his head to look at Ryan in the crowd and winked.

After being placed back into custody, Cheek was escorted back to the holding tank. He took a seat on the cold slab and lowered his head. The thought of never going home again was weighing heavy on his mind. The streets were his life, and those were the same streets that had turned their back on him. The game was officially over.

Hearing the loud knock on his holding cell door, Cheek looked up to see Detective Bradley standing at the window. He rose to his feet and moved towards him.

"You pussy motherfucker. You got some nerve getting me three life sentences and then coming back here to face me."

"Damn, dawg. I thought we were brothers." Detective Brad-ley smiled.

Cheek launched a glob of spit at the window and kicked it twice. "You're dead. That's on all I love."

"Oh, really? You might wanna watch your filthy mouth, be-cause I'm the same one that got this judge to place that three life sentences in the system as a twenty-five to thirty. Show some respect, motherfucker, 'cause it can easily switch back to the rest of your miserable life. Maybe when you come home this time, you won't have to do stupid things in order to be seen. I'll be waiting."

Watching Cheek crack a sly smile, Bradley turned around and walked off.

* * *

After meeting up with Bradley for his weekly payment, Ryan headed to Cheek's trial to end the bad talk of his long-term friend. To the public eyes, Cheek was never coming home. In Ryan's vision, he would be home sooner than everyone thought. It was already in motion.

As he slid his whip down the block, his phone began to vibrate. He slid it up to his ear and answered, "What's up?"

"Ryan, you need to get down to A-I Dupont Hospital. Faith is going into labor!" Markie-D yelled through the line.

Dropping the phone on his car floor, Ryan mashed the pedal, heading straight for the expressway.

* * *

Faith, A-I Dupont Hospital

"Push, Faith. We can see the baby's head. Push," the white female doctor said as Faith screamed at the top of her lungs.

The horrible feeling was the worst thing she'd ever experi-enced in her life. After a few moments of strong black girl power, she birthed a handsome 7 pound 4 ounce baby boy. His little cries sounded off through her ears as the doctors wrapped him up.

"Here's your little one, Mommy." The doctor handed him over to her.

"Oh my God. He looks just like him." Faith pouted her lips as her mom and dad shared a laugh.

"I think that's the way it's supposed to work, honey." Mrs. Anderson placed a light peck on her grandson's head.

Watching Ryan burst through the room, Faith looked up into his face and frowned. "I'm glad to see that you finally made it. Say hello to your son, Prince Royal."

Ignoring her ignorance, he slowly walked over and gently grabbed his seed. His bright skin was a reflection of his father's. His eyebrows were bushy, and his chubby hands said that he would grow to be a big and healthy child. The feeling of his own baby caused a new sense of life to grasp him. Prince was now his priority, a son that he could say was raised the correct way.

Walking over to Ryan, Markie-D patted him on the back. "Congratulations, son. Welcome to the family, young bull .If y'all excuse me and your mother, we're going to do some new shop-ping for my grandson." He smiled like it was the best day of his life.

"Thanks, Markie."

"Always."

They left Ryan and Faith alone in the hospital room. Faith cleared her throat. "So I'm guessing you're still not talking to me, huh?

"Faith, I don't have time to go through the dumb shit with you. I'm just happy to see my child. If you weren't always in your feelings, maybe we could be better. I'm just not trying to force it."

Faith was scared to see what her relationship with Ryan was coming to. In the past few months, he was getting so much money that he didn't care about anything they shared anymore. After meeting Precious, Faith became slightly jealous, which tossed Ryan in a defensive mode. She was his so-called business partner, but things just weren't looking right to the outside world. The couple who they witnessed become the most valuable in school became the worst two after having a horrible fall out.

"What do I have to do in order to see our family be close? 'Cause this isn't how I want us to be for Prince."

"We'll be okay. I just need to focus on handling my business and being a father. We don't have to be on good terms to raise our little one." Ryan placed a kiss on his son's cheek before handing him back to Faith.

"Business? Nigga, I'm talking about our family. Ever since you been running around with that little bitch Precious, your mind hasn't been correct. Are you sleeping with that girl, Ryan? Just let me know so I can accept that you don't love me any-more."

Looking at her with a stupid expression, he laughed. "See what I'm saying? I have a child by you. I give you whatever you want. I've stood by you through whatever. Precious is - "

"Your business partner. You can run that game on somebody else, Ryan. Let me ask you something. Do you think that selling dope and fucking hoes will last forever? No one will be by your side when they slam you in a prison cell like Cheek Raw. You're following in your dad's footsteps, but I'm sorry. He wasn't a dad to you."

"Shut the fuck up!" He pointed a finger in her face. "I've dealt with your stubborn-ass attitude for the past few months, and quite frankly, I'm tired of it. You're so stuck in your own ways that you don't even want me to handle the same duties that put the food on our plate. You're about to graduate, Faith. Are your mom and dad paying for that college education, or am I? Don't ever mention that my dad wasn't a good father, because I damn sho' do my part as a man."

Faith held onto Prince with tears in her eyes. "I only try to show you how much I love you. Since you first met me, I've given you nothing but loyalty. You treat me so wrong and I still stand here. I didn't ask you to get me pregnant, Ryan."

"And neither did I. But it's done, and my son is here, Faith. We are bonded, regardless of whatever we choose to do. Maybe we just need a break from each other. I don't want to be the blame for why you in your feelings, and it ain't happening in the near future either." Ryan was ready to end all the petty games.

"So what are you telling me to do from here?"

"Take care of my son while I'm in the stress making sure we survive every day. It's easy," Ryan said before turning to leave out the door.

At the end of the day, nothing was guaranteed. Since Cheek Raw was gone, Ryan had officially became the man within 120 days. He had to feed his pockets for the sake of his son and family. With Bradley keeping him off the radar, he reigned victory over all competition. Reckless and

Wicked were caught snooping a few times, but still and all, Ryan kept his distance. All he needed was the right chance to catch either one slipping the wrong way and it was over.

Chapter 18

Precious, the Opening of Club Royal, Philly

The loud round of applause in the building sounded off as Precious finished her light speech. The opening of hers and Ryan's new spot was a success. Not only did she pack the space to its five thousand person capacity, but she was able to get a few guests to show up also. It wasn't easy to get a singer like Jaquees to make a short stop for a single, but it was made possible thanks to the promoters she hired. They sponsored an entire event just for her effort. Teachers from the college she attended, students, and of course her family attended the opening as well.

Precious wore a beautiful black blouse that showed a little cleavage. She rocked a pair of black leather Gucci skintight pants and a pair of Roberto Cavalli high heels. Her makeup was bomb, and she was sure to keep a smile on her face with every person's hand she shook.

Ryan walked over and embraced her into a tight hug. "This is epic. I love it." he whispered in her ear ."You welcome." She placed a warm kiss on his cheek. I told you that we can pull it off. I see us prospering even more within the next few weeks. We have a lot of supporters."

"I see. All my people is running around here." Ryan took a second to gaze around.

The marble floors were glistening to perfection. VIP sections were loaded with leather couches and pillows for the classy level. The mini bar was stuffed with over sixty different types of drinks. The music was always gonna be the original R & B and hip hop. There was a dining section, and even a small porch were you could go and take a breather. Everything about Club Royal spelled elegance, and the crowd was surely enjoying it. After grabbing a few champagne flutes from the bartender's tray, Precious pulled Ryan over towards her parents.

"Mama, Dad!" she yelled out.

Her father was obviously a doctor or some type of lawyer. His apparel screamed rich, and he didn't look over the age of fifty. Her mother was a caramel-complexioned woman. Her eyes were chinky and she had the same dimples as Precious.

"Hey, darling," her father spoke first.

"Hi Dad, Mom. I want you to meet Ryan. He's the owner." Precious smiled.

"Hi Ryan. It's a pleasure to meet you, darling. My daugh-ter tells me that you have big dreams for yourself. I'm glad that she can be of assistance to you."

"Oh yes, ma'am. Your daughter is my best friend. It was so fun watching this project blossom. I don't think I could've did it without her." Ryan grinned from ear to ear. He was trying his best to put on the properly-educated man voice. It was a blessing he had never decided to get tattoos.

"She is very intelligent. Don't let her take your shine, man. She's too dang smart for herself sometimes," her dad said before shaking his hand.

Precious couldn't do anything but giggle. "You guys are too much. We have guests to attend to. Don't get too drunk." She grabbed Ryan's hand to pull him away.

"I see your parents have really good faith in you." He laughed.

"Yeah, fifty percent of their faith comes from talking me to death," she agreed.

After mingling and sharing a few drinks with their guests, the party was in effect. People shared laughs and dances. Even the elderly got a chance to come and show off a few old moves to school a young one down. The night began to pass and eventually everyone started to share their goodbyes and good nights.

Taking a seat at the bar, Ryan ordered a round of Ciroc vod-ka. After taking the shot to the head, he held up his finger for one more. The days that were going by filled Ryan with so much joy. Instead of the disasters and bad luck, he was receiving God's mercy to pass in the streets. All was being perfected daily. It was the reason he still held the position as number one. He deserved it.

Thinking about Precious, he smiled. She was the ultimate. Her skills were past amazing, and she was actually excited about helping him achieve something so beautiful. He only wished that Kimyetta was there to witness it. He had felt so down in regards to accomplishing things that he began to really feel that he wouldn't make it. Precious came into his life and switched those beliefs right out of him.

After downing his last shot, Ryan watched as Detective Bradley made his way over to the bar. He took a seat next to Ryan and ordered a beer.

"So how do you like your new place? It's nice."

"It's great. That's what happens when you hustle the right way," Ryan replied without looking at him.

Nodding his head, Bradley smirked. "From my under-stand-ing, you're the man in the spot now, son. I can't even swerve around Wilmington without hearing about you. Now I had to slide way over to Philly and see this new masterpiece of yours. The new price is fifty thousand every month, Ryan. Prices are rising because jail cells are getting emptier by the day. In order to skip past you and tackle the rest of your problems, I need you to pay the way you play."

Looking at him with a pathetic expression, Ryan smiled. "No problem, Bradley."

In the end, Ryan knew that there was no other way around it. A cop would be a cop, whether dirty or clean. All you could do was master the plots until you could take advantage.

Reaching in his coat pocket, Bradley pulled a small black card from his pocket, sliding over to Ryan. He rose to his feet.

"I respect your hustle, kid. You've proved me wrong about you. Be there or kill yourself. You wanted your chance. You got it." He turned to leave.

Ryan looked down at the black business card. He stared at the stamped letters M.C. on the front, flashing back to the day he had cleared out Cheek's safe. The photo memory of the card bounced through his mind. As Bradley walked out of the door, he picked the card up and placed it into his pocket. He finished the last of his drink, rose to his feet, and headed to find Precious.

He located her by the DJ booth. She was crowded up with DJ, Sekoya, and a few others. Judging from the bottles in their hands, drinks were being passed for free, the same way it had been going since the doors opened.

"What's good, y'all? Precious, I just came to let you know that I was about head out. I have an important day tomorrow, and I wanna be sure that I get some rest."

"Alright, sweetie. I'll call you tomorrow before I come over." She kissed his cheek.

After showing his best friend DJ some love, he hugged Sekoya and she placed a kiss on his cheek also. "Goodnight, y'all."

"Later, bro," DJ answered for them all.

* * *

Once at his three bedroom house, Ryan quickly made his way inside. Philly was comfortable, especially when he could run to Delaware and apply his pressure where it was needed.

He headed straight for the closet in his bedroom and opened his large safe. He pulled out the card. He removed the one from his pocket and analyzed them both. They were the exact same. The marking. The color. The symbol. They both also shared the same address. If Bradley gave him one, and the other was found in Cheek's safe, it was clear that not just anyone was capable of having one.

Bradley's remark replayed back in his mind. "Be there or kill yourself. You said you wanted your chance. You got it."

It was surely something that he was going to do alone. If this was an opportunity like Bradley presented. He was going to take it and prosper to be bigger than the next.

After closing his safe, he grabbed his phone and called Pre-cious's number.

"Hey Ryan."

"Wassup, ma? I need you to do me a favor."

"Anything," she said a little too quickly.

"Pick me up a suit from the clothing store, please. All black, and make sure its name brand."

"No problem, love. I'll bring it when I come over to-morrow."

"Cool." He hung up.

The time to reign supreme was thick in the air. Ryan had waited so long to make it to the top, and this time he was sure that a king would be crowned for good.

Chapter 19

Ryan's spot, North Philly, 10:48 p.m.

"How do I look?" Ryan asked as Precious rubbed his wavy hair.

"You look handsome. Like a boss," she responded.

Checking himself out in the mirror for a second, he noticed that she was staring at him. "What, ma?"

"Nothing. I'm just happy to be around you. I can't help it."

He kissed her passionately and held her cheek. "Thank you. For everything."

"You're welcome. Now go ahead and get out of here so you won't be late. I'll be waiting for you to come back." She blushed.

"That's a bet, ma."

After grabbing his trench coat, he tucked his Glock 32 hand-gun into his shoulder holster and left out the door. He hopped in his Infinti truck, pulled out, and headed for his destination.

* * *

Wilmington Delaware, 11:36

Randy's sports bar

Hopping out of his car, Ryan took a deep breath and headed for the door of the small business. The parking lot was nearly empty besides a few exotic cars that sat a few feet away from each other.

Once he got to the entrance, he was stopped by the two large security officers.

"You sure you at the right place, man?"

Ryan pulled the card from his pocket. The man stared at it be-fore placing the golden ticket back into his palm.

"You need to talk to Lizzy at the bar. She can help you," he stated humbly before stepping out of his way.

Nodding, Ryan continued to make his way inside. Only four people mingled throughout the joint. One man played pool by himself while two women danced with each other to the slow music that was playing. The next person was an older Spanish-looking woman who sipped a glass of wine smoothly. Her eyes landed on Ryan when he walked through the spot, but he didn't let that detour his mission.

When he got to the counter, he stared at the country-raised white girl. Her teeth were spread further apart than a field goal. Her breasts were extra huge, saggy titties that hung down to her stomach. A black mole rested over her lip, and her blonde hair was wrapped in a bun.

"Hey hun? Can I get you something to drink?"

"No thank you. I was told that I need to see Lizzy." Ryan slid the card towards her.

Looking down at it, her entire facial expression flopped. "You sure you don't want a drink, baby?"

"I'm positive," he stated a little more sternly.

"Okay, follow me. She removed her apron and headed for the back.

She moved towards a door and opened it. "Down the stairs."

As Ryan stepped through the threshold, she closed the door behind them and headed down the dark staircase. Upon reaching the bottom, they approached a steel door.

She turned around to stop him. Her face became serious, like a lion about to jump on his prey. "Listen, honey bun, don't speak unless you're spoken to. Never let anything that happens in here leave. It's the rules. Just follow them and you'll win."

Ryan nodded in agreement. She turned around and placed three sharp knocks on the steel. After a few seconds passed, the sliding flap opened, revealing a man's eyes

"Who the hell is he?"

"How about you open the door and find out?" Lizzy said sar-castically.

The latches clicked. The door to the room slowly opened and a bulky white guy with a bulletproof vest stepped out.

"I've never seen him before."

Ryan looked at him with a blank expression. He was antici-pating something wrong to happen, and this big guy would surely be the first one to receive a slug.

"Who sent you here?" the man asked.

"I'm not a fucking snitch. I got the card and I'm here," he re-sponded, feeling the aggravation about to boil.

"Wait here." The door was shut back in his face.

"Well, this is where my job ends, baby. I'll see you again when you leave out, cutie." She pinched Ryan's cheek before walking back up the steps.

After a few seconds, the locks twisted again and this time the pussy security man was with another white boy. This one looked totally different. His fingers sported a ring and watch that could easily go for a hundred grand. His suit was fitted perfectly and his hair would remind you of the actor Mark Wahlberg.

"Who sent you, kid?"

Ryan handed him the card. He raised his eyes to look back at Ryan. "You look familiar. What's your name?

"Ryan."

Raising an eyebrow, he cracked a wry smile. "Welcome, Ryan, I'm Richard." He stepped to the side so he could enter. The bodyguard stood back at his post while the two of them headed inside the clean room.

As they made their way around the corner, all eyes landed on Ryan. A huge meeting table sat in the center of this huge blue lighted area. There were about twelve others who occupied chairs around the space, and Richard wasted no time taking his seat.

Spotting the last chair, Ryan walked smoothly over and took a seat without saying a word.

Looking at his timepiece, Richard smiled. "I'm glad that you all could make it. Welcome to the Midnight Cartel."

TO BE CONTINUED...
Midnight Cartel 2: Envy and Greed
Coming Soon

Submission Guideline

Submit the first three chapters of your completed manuscript to ldpsubmissions@gmail.com, subject line: Your book's title. The manuscript must be in a .doc file and sent as an attachment. Document should be in Times New Roman, double spaced and in size 12 font. Also, provide your synopsis and full contact information. If sending multiple submissions, they must each be in a separate email.

Have a story but no way to send it electronically? You can still submit to LDP/Ca$h Presents. Send in the first three chapters, written or typed, of your completed manuscript to:

LDP: Submissions Dept
Po Box 870494
Mesquite, Tx 75187

DO NOT send original manuscript. Must be a duplicate.

Provide your synopsis and a cover letter containing your full contact information.

Thanks for considering LDP and Ca$h Presents.

Coming Soon from Lock Down Publications/Ca$h Presents

BOW DOWN TO MY GANGSTA

By **Ca$h**

TORN BETWEEN TWO

By **Coffee**

BLOOD STAINS OF A SHOTTA **III**

By **Jamaica**

STEADY MOBBIN **III**

By **Marcellus Allen**

BLOOD OF A BOSS **VI**

SHADOWS OF THE GAME II

By **Askari**

LOYAL TO THE GAME **IV**

By **T.J. & Jelissa**

A DOPEBOY'S PRAYER **II**

By **Eddie "Wolf" Lee**

IF LOVING YOU IS WRONG... **III**

By **Jelissa**

TRUE SAVAGE **VII**

MIDNIGHT CARTEL

DOPE BOY MAGIC II

By **Chris Green**

BLAST FOR ME **III**

DUFFLE BAG CARTEL **IV**

HEARTLESS GOON **IV**

A SAVAGE DOPEBOY II

DRUG LORDS II

By **Ghost**

A HUSTLER'S DECEIT III

KILL ZONE **II**

BAE BELONGS TO ME III

SOUL OF A MONSTER III

By **Aryanna**

THE COST OF LOYALTY **III**

By **Kweli**

THE SAVAGE LIFE III

By **J-Blunt**

KING OF NEW YORK V

COKE KINGS IV

BORN HEARTLESS III

By **T.J. Edwards**

GORILLAZ IN THE BAY V

De'Kari

THE STREETS ARE CALLING II

Duquie Wilson

KINGPIN KILLAZ IV

STREET KINGS III

PAID IN BLOOD III

CARTEL KILLAZ III

Hood Rich

SINS OF A HUSTLA II

ASAD

Chris Green

TRIGGADALE III
Elijah R. Freeman
KINGZ OF THE GAME V
Playa Ray
SLAUGHTER GANG IV
RUTHLESS HEART II
By Willie Slaughter
THE HEART OF A SAVAGE II
By Jibril Williams
FUK SHYT II
By Blakk Diamond
THE DOPEMAN'S BODYGAURD II
By Tranay Adams
TRAP GOD II
By Troublesome
YAYO II
A SHOOTER'S AMBITION II
By S. Allen
GHOST MOB
Stilloan Robinson
KINGPIN DREAMS
By Paper Boi Rari
CREAM
By Yolanda Moore
SON OF A DOPE FIEND II
By Renta
FOREVER GANGSTA II

By Adrian Dulan

LOYALTY AIN'T PROMISED

By Keith Williams

THE PRICE YOU PAY FOR LOVE

By Destiny Skai

THE LIFE OF A HOOD STAR

By Rashia Wilson

TOE TAGZ II

By Ah'Million

Available Now

RESTRAINING ORDER **I & II**

By **CA$H & Coffee**

LOVE KNOWS NO BOUNDARIES **I II & III**

By **Coffee**

RAISED AS A GOON I, II, III & IV

BRED BY THE SLUMS I, II, III

BLAST FOR ME I & II

ROTTEN TO THE CORE I II III

A BRONX TALE I, II, III

DUFFEL BAG CARTEL I II III

HEARTLESS GOON

A SAVAGE DOPEBOY

HEARTLESS GOON I II III

DRUG LORDS

By **Ghost**

LAY IT DOWN **I & II**

LAST OF A DYING BREED

BLOOD STAINS OF A SHOTTA I & II

By **Jamaica**

LOYAL TO THE GAME

LOYAL TO THE GAME II

LOYAL TO THE GAME III

LIFE OF SIN I, II III

By **TJ & Jelissa**

BLOODY COMMAS I & II

SKI MASK CARTEL I II & III

KING OF NEW YORK I II,III IV

RISE TO POWER I II III

COKE KINGS I II III

BORN HEARTLESS I II

By **T.J. Edwards**

IF LOVING HIM IS WRONG…I & II

LOVE ME EVEN WHEN IT HURTS I II III

By **Jelissa**

WHEN THE STREETS CLAP BACK I & II III

By **Jibril Williams**

A DISTINGUISHED THUG STOLE MY HEART I II & III

LOVE SHOULDN'T HURT I II III IV

RENEGADE BOYS I II III IV

By **Meesha**

A GANGSTER'S CODE I &, II III

A GANGSTER'S SYN I II III

THE SAVAGE LIFE I II

By J-Blunt

PUSH IT TO THE LIMIT

By **Bre' Hayes**

BLOOD OF A BOSS **I, II, III, IV, V**

SHADOWS OF THE GAME

By **Askari**

THE STREETS BLEED MURDER **I, II & III**

THE HEART OF A GANGSTA I II& III

By **Jerry Jackson**

CUM FOR ME

CUM FOR ME 2

CUM FOR ME 3

CUM FOR ME 4

CUM FOR ME 5

An **LDP Erotica Collaboration**

BRIDE OF A HUSTLA **I II & II**

THE FETTI GIRLS **I, II& III**

CORRUPTED BY A GANGSTA I, II III, IV

BLINDED BY HIS LOVE

By **Destiny Skai**

WHEN A GOOD GIRL GOES BAD

By **Adrienne**

THE COST OF LOYALTY I II

By Kweli

A GANGSTER'S REVENGE **I II III & IV**

THE BOSS MAN'S DAUGHTERS

THE BOSS MAN'S DAUGHTERS II

THE BOSSMAN'S DAUGHTERS III

THE BOSSMAN'S DAUGHTERS IV

THE BOSS MAN'S DAUGHTERS **V**

A SAVAGE LOVE **I & II**

BAE BELONGS TO ME I II

A HUSTLER'S DECEIT I, II, III

WHAT BAD BITCHES DO I, II, III

SOUL OF A MONSTER I II

KILL ZONE

By **Aryanna**

A KINGPIN'S AMBITON

A KINGPIN'S AMBITION **II**

I MURDER FOR THE DOUGH

By **Ambitious**

TRUE SAVAGE

TRUE SAVAGE II

TRUE SAVAGE **III**

TRUE SAVAGE **IV**

TRUE SAVAGE **V**

TRUE SAVAGE **VI**

DOPE BOY MAGIC

MIDNIGHT CARTEL

By **Chris Green**

A DOPEBOY'S PRAYER

By **Eddie "Wolf" Lee**

THE KING CARTEL **I, II & III**

By **Frank Gresham**

THESE NIGGAS AIN'T LOYAL **I, II & III**

By **Nikki Tee**

GANGSTA SHYT **I II &III**

By **CATO**

THE ULTIMATE BETRAYAL

By **Phoenix**

BOSS'N UP **I , II & III**

By **Royal Nicole**

I LOVE YOU TO DEATH

By Destiny J

I RIDE FOR MY HITTA

I STILL RIDE FOR MY HITTA

By **Misty Holt**

LOVE & CHASIN' PAPER

By **Qay Crockett**

TO DIE IN VAIN

SINS OF A HUSTLA

By **ASAD**

BROOKLYN HUSTLAZ

By **Boogsy Morina**

BROOKLYN ON LOCK I & II

By **Sonovia**

GANGSTA CITY

By **Teddy Duke**

A DRUG KING AND HIS DIAMOND I & II III

A DOPEMAN'S RICHES

HER MAN, MINE'S TOO I, II

CASH MONEY HO'S

By Nicole Goosby

TRAPHOUSE KING **I II & III**

KINGPIN KILLAZ I II III

STREET KINGS I II

PAID IN BLOOD **I II**

CARTEL KILLAZ I II

By **Hood Rich**

LIPSTICK KILLAH **I, II, III**

CRIME OF PASSION I II & III

By **Mimi**

STEADY MOBBN' **I, II, III**

By **Marcellus Allen**

WHO SHOT YA **I, II, III**

SON OF A DOPE FIEND

Renta

GORILLAZ IN THE BAY **I II III IV**

DE'KARI

TRIGGADALE I II

Elijah R. Freeman

GOD BLESS THE TRAPPERS I, II, III

THESE SCANDALOUS STREETS I, II, III

FEAR MY GANGSTA I, II, III

THESE STREETS DON'T LOVE NOBODY I, II

BURY ME A G I, II, III, IV, V

A GANGSTA'S EMPIRE I, II, III, IV

THE DOPEMAN'S BODYGAURD

Tranay Adams

THE STREETS ARE CALLING

Duquie Wilson

MARRIED TO A BOSS... I II III

By Destiny Skai & Chris Green

KINGZ OF THE GAME I II III IV

Playa Ray

SLAUGHTER GANG I II III

RUTHLESS HEART

By Willie Slaughter

THE HEART OF A SAVAGE

By Jibril Williams

FUK SHYT

By Blakk Diamond

DON'T F#CK WITH MY HEART I II

By Linnea

ADDICTED TO THE DRAMA I II III

By Jamila

YAYO

A SHOOTER'S AMBITION

By S. Allen

TRAP GOD

By Troublesome

FOREVER GANGSTA

By Adrian Dulan

TOE TAGZ

Chris Green

By Ah'Million

BOOKS BY LDP'S CEO, CA$H

TRUST IN NO MAN

TRUST IN NO MAN 2

TRUST IN NO MAN 3

BONDED BY BLOOD

SHORTY GOT A THUG

THUGS CRY

THUGS CRY 2

THUGS CRY 3

TRUST NO BITCH

TRUST NO BITCH 2

TRUST NO BITCH 3

TIL MY CASKET DROPS

RESTRAINING ORDER

RESTRAINING ORDER 2

IN LOVE WITH A CONVICT

Coming Soon

BONDED BY BLOOD 2

BOW DOWN TO MY GANGSTA

www.ingramcontent.com/pod-product-compliance
Lightning Source LLC
Chambersburg PA
CBHW070509260626
47161CB00004B/1501